ST. JOHN'S LUTHERAN
ELEMENTARY SCHOOL
"For a Christ-Centered Education"
3521 Linda Vista Ave.
Napa, California

BOOKS BY

JOHN W. CHAMBERS

Fritzi's Winter

Finder

Showdown at Apple Hill

Showdown at Apple Hill

John W. Chambers

SHOWDOWN AT APPLE HILL

New York ATHENEUM 1982

Library of Congress Cataloging in Publication Data

Chambers, John W., 1933–
Showdown at Apple Hill.

Summary: Trying to save a local home for retarded children Jenny and Billy Martin discover they are also involved in a hunt for the lost bank-robbery loot of the Quarry gang.
[1. Mystery and detective stories. 2. New England—Fiction]
I. Title.
PZ7.C3563Sh [Fic] 81-10774
ISBN 0-689-30897-3 AACR2

Copyright © 1982 by John Chambers
All rights reserved
Published simultaneously in Canada by
McClelland & Stewart, Ltd.
Composition by American–Stratford Graphic Services, Inc.
Brattleboro, Vermont
Manufactured by Fairfield Graphics, Fairfield, Pennsylvania
Designed by Harry Ford
First Edition

To John

Contents

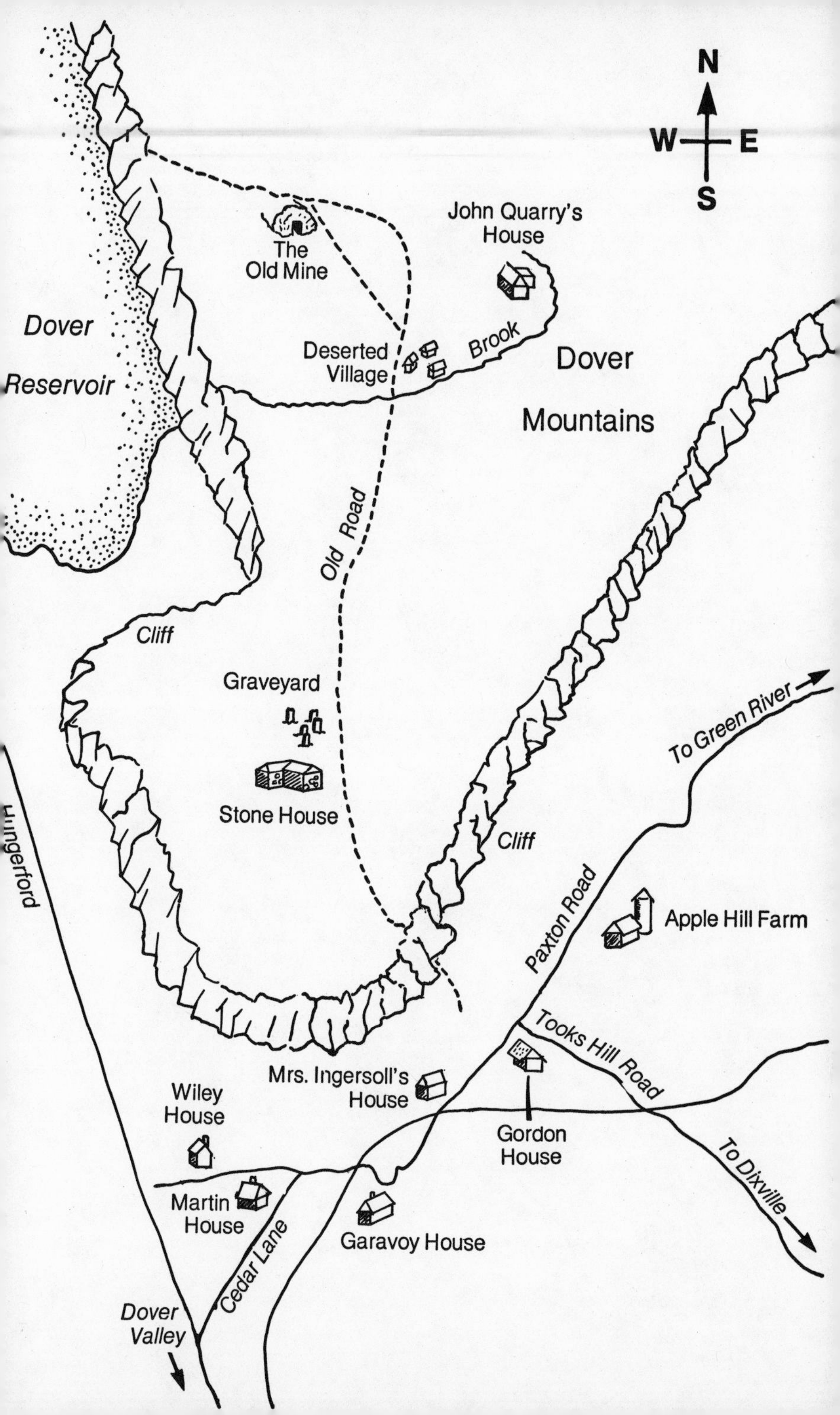
N
W
E
S
John Quarry's House
The Old Mine
Dover Reservoir
Deserted Village
Brook
Dover Mountains
Old Road
Cliff
Graveyard
Stone House
Cliff
To Green River
ungerford
Paxton Road
Apple Hill Farm
Tooks Hill Road
Mrs. Ingersoll's House
Wiley House
Gordon House
To Dixville
Martin House
Cedar Lane
Garavoy House
Dover Valley

Showdown at Apple Hill

1 The Quarry Gang

JENNY MARTIN stood on the back porch, watching her dog, Skipper. It was a bright, sparkling September morning, and with the school week over, two days of freedom stretched before her. She looked across the road, her eyes scaling the slope until they reached the sheer cliff that marked the southernmost extension of Dover Mountain. There was something harsh and forbidding in its aspect; something wild and untamed. She had been fascinated by it ever since her family had moved to Dover Valley in late August, but up until now, there had been little time for anything but getting settled and adjusting to a new school. Now all that was behind her, and tomorrow she and Billy were going to climb Dover Mountain and visit the graveyard, the deserted village, and the old mine. She was looking forward to it. She studied the cliff face a few seconds longer. Then she called Skipper, and shooing him ahead of her, stepped inside. Her mother was fixing breakfast.

"Is Billy up?" she asked as she saw Jenny.

"He'll be down in a minute," Jenny replied. At eleven Billy was a year and a half younger than she was, but they got along surprisingly well. "Did Daddy go yet?"

"He left at six. He probably won't be back until after supper."

Jenny nodded and sat down. Mr. Martin had driven to Long Island to close their beach house. Originally he had intended to take Jenny and Billy, but he had changed his mind. Jenny was just as glad.

"Here's Billy."

As Billy hurried into the room and sat down, Mrs. Martin served the bacon, eggs, and toast, while Jenny poured orange juice and milk. They ate rapidly. Only when Jenny and Billy were almost finished did Mrs. Martin ask if they had any plans for the day.

"We're going to Debbie Wiley's house," Jenny replied.

"Will you be back for lunch, or do you want to take sandwiches?"

Jenny glanced at her brother. "Sandwiches, if that would be all right."

"I'll make them up now. I'll be going out about eleven."

"Where are you going?" Billy asked.

"Apple Hill Farm. I want to arrange to get fresh milk and vegetables there."

"Isn't that the place where they have the retarded people?" Jenny asked.

"Yes. You ought to walk up there. I hear they're looking for kids to help out. You could earn some pocket money."

"Maybe we will."

Getting up from the table, Jenny took her plate and glass over to the sink and washed them. Then she ran upstairs, and after making her bed, tidied her room and put away her Barbie dolls. Although most of her friends had given up Barbies years before, she had kept hers because they made good models for which to design clothes, and designing clothes was one of her favorite activities.

When she finished, she and Billy collected their sandwiches and started down Paxton Road toward the Wiley house. Skipper ran along beside them at first, but he soon wandered off to hunt through the woods that bordered the road on either side. They were turning into the Wiley driveway when Drew Wiley, who was Billy's age, spotted them and ran to meet them.

"Guess what?" he called excitedly. "Dad says Kurt Heineken just got out of jail. They think he's coming back here."

"Who's Kurt Heineken?"

"You don't know?" Drew stared at Billy and Jenny in amazement. "Haven't you ever heard about the Quarry gang?"

They both shook their heads. Drew stared a moment longer. Then he turned to his sister Debbie, who had just come up to them. "They don't know about the Quarry gang."

"How would we know about the Quarry gang?" Billy protested. "We only just moved here."

Drew was unimpressed. "Heck, I thought everybody knew about the Quarry gang. It was in all the papers. Especially when they had the shoot-out. People talk about it all the time."

"No one talked to us. Where did they have this shoot-out?"

Drew turned to his sister. "You tell them, Debbie."

Debbie frowned at her brother, casting a quick glance in the direction of the house. Mrs. Wiley had been standing on the doorstep a few seconds earlier, but she was no longer in sight. Reassured, Debbie turned to Jenny and Billy. "We aren't supposed to talk about it," she explained. "Drew should have kept his mouth shut. Dad doesn't want people to get upset or anything."

"Why would people get upset?"

"Kurt Heineken was always in trouble, and he made a lot of threats when they sent him to jail. Dad was the one who arrested him."

"How?"

"It was just after he got on the force. You see, Ed Quarry and his gang lived back in the hills between here and Hungerford. There were a whole lot of robberies, and no one could figure out who was doing it. Then one day Miles MacIntosh caught the gang robbing his house when he and his wife came home early, and the men killed him and wounded Mrs. MacIntosh. I guess they thought she was dead, too, but she wasn't, and she told the sheriff who had shot her and killed her husband."

"Was that when they had the shoot-out?"

"Yes. Three of the gang were killed, and Dad arrested Kurt Heineken a little later. Ed Quarry got away."

"Did they finally catch him?"

"Not for a long time. Then Dad got a tip one day, and they found him in the old stone house next to the graveyard on Dover Mountain."

"Did they send him to jail?"

"They didn't have a chance," Drew interrupted. "He was dead when they found him."

"Who killed him?"

"Dad thinks he shot himself. He had a pistol in his hand, and there was no sign of anyone else."

"How long ago was it?"

"A long time. I wasn't born then."

"It was twelve years ago," Debbie said firmly, sneaking another quick glance toward the door. "The reason Dad thinks Heineken will come back here is that hardly any of what was stolen has ever turned up. Dad thinks there must be a lot of money hidden somewhere, and he believes Heineken knows where it is."

"I'll bet your father's kind of worried if Heineken's what you say he is, and he's the one who arrested him," Billy commented. "I would be."

"Dad's not scared of Kurt Heineken," Drew assured him. "Dad's arrested lots of guys. He just doesn't want people to get all stirred up about it."

"You shouldn't have said anything, Drew," Debbie repeated with another uneasy glance at the house.

"We'll keep our mouths shut," Jenny assured her. "We both promise. Right, Billy?"

Billy nodded, and for a time they were silent. Then Jenny suggested they visit Liz Gordon, who lived a mile up Paxton Road from the junction where the Martin house was located. Liz was in Jenny's and Debbie's class at school, and although Jenny barely knew her, she liked her and wanted to get to know her better. So Debbie ran to the house to tell her mother where she and Drew were going. Then they started up Paxton Road.

Paxton Road had been dirt-surfaced until five years before, and it still had the character of a country lane. Actually it was a shortcut through the Dover Hills, but traffic was comparatively light, since it was too twisty and narrow for trucks. After passing the Cedar Lane junction, the road climbed precipitously, and the four of them were puffing when they emerged from the "S" curve and passed the Garavoy house. Wes Garavoy, the eldest of the two bachelor brothers, was chopping wood in the yard, and he and Billy exchanged a wave.

"How do you know Wes Garavoy?" Drew asked, as soon as they were out of earshot.

"He cut himself one day when he was chopping firewood on the hill back of our house, and I helped him bandage it and called Dr. Simmons for him," Billy said.

"Do you know his brother, too?"

"Lee? Sure."

"What are they like?"

"They're like anybody else. I like them."

"People say they're strange. They get drunk a lot."

"Maybe, but I've never seen them drinking. They know a lot about the woods. Wes is the one who told me about the deserted village on top of Dover Mountain."

"He *would* know about that."

"What do you mean?" Billy asked, glancing at Debbie.

For a moment Debbie remained silent. Then she turned to Billy. "Some people thought the Garavoys were tied into the Quarry gang."

Billy shook his head. "I don't see it. Wes and Lee go their own way. They're stubborn, and they can be rough, but they're straight. Wes told me once that he was offered a lot of money for his house and turned it down. I asked him why, and he said *to spite people.* He said there was no way anybody was going to buy out him and Lee, so they'd better get used to having the Garavoys around. He said money wasn't as important as doing what you wanted to do."

"They still might have been tied in with the Quarrys."

"If they were, they sure didn't get any of the money."

They had reached the Gordon house now. As they approached it, they looked hopefully for signs of activity, but there were none. A futile knock on the front door and a check of the garage confirmed their suspicion that the Gordons were away.

"What do we do now?" Debbie asked as they stood looking at the empty house.

"Why don't we go to Apple Hill Farm?" Jenny suggested.

"Why go there?"

"Mom said I might be able to get a job there for after school. You might be able to get one, too."

"What makes you think they're hiring people?"

"Mom said they were. Come on! We can at least ask."

Debbie looked at her brother. "What do you think, Drew?"

"I'm with Jenny."

"Let's go then," Jenny said.

Calling Skipper, she walked out to the road and started off. Debbie hesitated, then making up her mind, ran ahead and fell into step beside Jenny, the two boys bringing up the rear.

2 Apple Hill Farm

Apple Hill Farm was a mile down Paxton Road from the junction with Tooks Hill Road. On the way Debbie told the others what she knew about the Farm. It had been started ten years before on property owned by the Carey family. Mrs. Carey, who had been extremely wealthy, had given eighty-five acres and the farm buildings on them to the Apple Hill Foundation. Since then the Farm had been gradually expanding, putting up buildings as money became available and adding bits and pieces of acreage.

"Who runs it?" Jenny asked.

"Mr. Carrington. He's the director. His son graduated from Dover High last year. Do you know Diane Drake?"

Jenny shook her head. "I know who she is, but I've never talked to her."

"Her family works at Apple Hill. It's funny. There's a lot of feeling in Dover Valley against Apple Hill."

"Why?"

"I don't know. I've heard my parents talking about it. Part of it is that Apple Hill doesn't pay taxes. Then, too, some people don't like the idea of having the retarded kids here. There was trouble last year."

"What kind of trouble?"

"People said that one of the retarded kids attacked a little girl. Mr. Carrington denied it."

"What does your father say?"

"He agrees with Mr. Carrington. He thinks it was a set-up."

"Why?"

"When he tried to question the little girl, she wouldn't answer him, and her family gave him a real hard time. He thinks the people who are trying to get rid of Apple Hill planned the whole thing."

They had arrived at the entrance now. Passing between the two stone pillars that marked it, they started up the long driveway. The farm buildings were well back from the main road and were hidden by a grove of spruce. When they finally came into view, Jenny was surprised at their number and variety. In addition to the usual stock barns and silos, there were several large sheds, and on the hillside overlooking the farm, two long dormitories and several houses with an assortment of smaller sheds of varying sizes and shapes. A small brook ran behind the barns, and it was dammed in several places, forming ponds for ducks and geese.

"This place is really big," Billy muttered, looking around him. "How many retarded people do they have here?"

"Dad says about a hundred and twenty," Debbie replied. She glanced at Jenny. "What do we do now?"

"Let's see if we can find somebody to talk to about jobs."

Jenny started toward the building directly in front of her, but she had taken only a few steps when Skipper, who had been running through the sheep meadow on their right, began to bark excitedly. Apparently he had wandered too close to a pair of lambs, and the ewes had closed in on him unobserved and had cornered him against a watering trough. He was barking ferociously, trying to bluff them into keeping their distance, but the bluff wasn't working. Jenny ran to the fence and started to climb it, but before she had reached the top, a boy who seemed to be in his teens ran over, stick in hand, and began to wave it threateningly in Skipper's direction. Jenny shouted as she reached the ground and sprinted toward the boy, but a tall black man with an Afro haircut was ahead of her. Jenny came to a stop and watched, while Skipper scuttled away to safety. Finally the man looked up at her and smiled.

"Hi," he called. "I'm Tom Drake, and this is Simon Wells. Do you live around here?"

"We live in the Cruikshank house," Jenny replied. "My name's Jenny Martin. I ride the school bus with your daughter."

"Glad to meet you, Jenny. Simon here was just trying to chase your dog out of trouble, weren't you, Simon?"

The boy smiled and nodded vigorously. Looking at him more closely, Jenny guessed that he was in his late teens. He was nice-looking in spite of a slackness in his features, and his open, friendly smile was immediately winning.

The others had come up, and Jenny introduced them. After the introductions, she explained why they had come and asked to whom they should speak about jobs.

"You've come to the right party," Mr. Drake replied with a smile. "I'll tell you what we'll do. Let me show you around the place, and then we'll go back to my house and talk."

For the next half-hour they walked around the farm with Skipper trailing them closely. They saw the cow barns, the dairy, the sheep pens, and the chicken yard, and then they were taken through the bakery and the handicraft shops. Everywhere they saw campers, as the retarded boys and girls were called, hard at work with one or more counselors working with them and helping them. When they would come into a room, the campers would look up and greet them with smiles and the slightly extravagant gestures to which Jenny and the others were rapidly becoming accustomed.

A highlight of the tour was the bakery, which was rich with the smell of baking bread. A batch of banana bread had just come out of the oven, and they tasted the fresh bread with the campers who had made it. Then they went on to the woodworking shop where five campers were working with a counselor, shaping table and chair legs. Billy and Drew were particularly fascinated, and Mr. Drake explained that the counselor did the designing and drew up the plans from which the campers worked.

"You see," he explained, "this whole program was evolved by Mr. Carrington from European models. The idea behind it is self-help. The campers, guided by the counselors, do virtually all the work on the farm. Of course, the money we make from the sale of produce and handicrafts doesn't begin to pay all the bills. We rely on grants and donations for that. It does pay for part of it, though, and the campers know that, and they're proud of it. They're not extra weight around here, and there's a lot of satisfaction in that feeling when you've never had it before."

The tour ended with the sewing crafts shed, and here it was Jenny and Debbie who could hardly be dragged away. Although Jenny had been sewing for some time, she had never tried to knit, and she and Debbie were amazed at the speed and dexterity of the knitters. The needlepoint, too, intrigued them. Two girls were making chair seats, following an intricate floral pattern. They paid close attention and made few mistakes. Jenny motioned Mr. Drake aside and asked how, if they were retarded, they were able to do such precise and exacting work.

"The fact is, there isn't any one level of retardation," he explained. "Whereas some retarded people have little physical control, others have as much as you and I. We have all levels here, although it's true that most of our campers are pretty good with their hands. We're just not equipped to handle the ones that aren't. What we do is evaluate each camper's abilities, and then choose jobs each can learn to do. That's why we need part-time counselors in addition to the full-time staff. Even the best of our campers need supervision and encouragement."

"Would that be what we'd be doing, working as part-time counselors?"

"Right. Let's walk over to my house where we can talk."

The Drake house was a large frame building with green shutters and a chimney at either end. Jenny suspected from the size that it doubled as a dormitory for campers, and that proved to be the case. Turning the corner past a chimney, they stepped through a screen door into a large, roomy kitchen. Mrs. Drake soon joined them, and they quickly settled around the kitchen table, feasting on freshly baked cookies and milk.

"I hear you kids ride the same school bus as Diane," Mrs. Drake observed presently.

"We do. Is Diane around?"

Mrs. Drake shook her head. "She's out with some campers on a picnic. She should be back before too long."

"Does she work as a counselor?" Billy asked.

"Sometimes. We're short-staffed right now, and she helps out when she can. She's good with the campers."

"So you kids would like to work for us." Mr. Drake had poured himself a cup of coffee and was holding the cup and saucer in his lap. "What can you do?"

The suddenness of the question startled them, and no one spoke for perhaps a minute. Then Jenny mentioned her sewing and designing.

"Maybe I could work with the campers in the doll shop," she suggested.

"I'm pretty good at ceramics," Debbie chimed in. "I've been making pots for two years now."

Mr. Drake nodded and turned to Billy. "What about you, Billy?"

Billy stared back at him uneasily. "I like woodwork, but I'm not as good at it as Jenny is at sewing. I think I could learn, though. I think I could learn fast."

"And you, Drew?"

"I'd like to work with Billy."

Mr. Drake nodded, glancing at his wife. "What do you think, Georgia?"

"I'm for it, but of course we'll have to talk to Mr.

Carrington." She looked down at the table, frowning slightly. "You see, we're very concerned about public relations right now. The main reason we're hiring local kids is that we want people to learn about Apple Hill and find out what it's really like. It's the only way we can fight the people who don't want us here, and there seem to be a lot of them."

"I wouldn't say that, Georgia, " Mr. Drake said quickly, setting his coffee cup on the table. "The people who are working against us are a minority."

"They may be a minority, but they make a lot of noise. They've been making a lot of charges, and they're hurting us. Because of them, it looks as if we may lose our state grant, and they've been going after our big contributors, telling them that the community doesn't want us here. They've offered to buy us out at a good price, and some of the trustees think we should take the money and relocate. It seems easy to them. They don't know the work that has gone into building up this place."

"They know. They just don't think our future in Dover Valley looks too promising." Mr. Drake watched his wife, then turned to the others. "I'll tell you what. Let's say that unless I call you, you'll start on Monday and work three days a week."

"How much will we be paid?" Drew asked.

"We'll work that out, but what I'm going to suggest is that we'll provide your families with dairy products and vegetables in season, and they can pay you what they'd usually pay in the market. Is that fair?"

They all nodded.

"Okay. Ask your parents tonight. If I don't hear from you, and if I don't call you, I'll expect to see you on Monday. I'll talk to your parents early next week, and we'll make the financial arrangements."

"Hi, everybody!"

They all looked up as Diane Drake stepped through the screen door. Mr. Drake quickly performed the introductions, and Diane sat down at the table and told them about the picnic. She was a lively girl and she soon had them in stitches with her account of the picnic, which had been highlighted by her sitting unintentionally on the hard-boiled eggs. Apparently the campers had enjoyed the outing immensely, and Diane was particularly pleased that a girl of her own age, who had been quite withdrawn recently, had come out of her shell and participated fully. Finally the Martins and the Wileys stood up to go, and Skipper, who had been sleeping under the table, crawled out to join them.

"Want to take the rest of the cookies?" Mrs. Drake asked.

Jenny shook her head. "No, thanks. We've got sandwiches with us."

"Monday then?"

Jenny looked at Mr. Drake and smiled. "Monday."

3 On Dover Mountain

JENNY and Billy ate early the next morning. The night before they had told their parents their intention of working at Apple Hill Farm, and the Martins had been delighted. In answer to Jenny's question, Mr. Martin had explained that local opposition to the Farm was led by Mr. Crabtree, a former Selectman, who owned a large tract of land just up the road from Apple Hill. He had convinced a number of his fellow landowners that property values were being lowered by the Farm, and that it was to their interest to see it change hands. Also, and even worse, he and the others who opposed Apple Hill had started a whispering campaign, saying that sooner or later violence would erupt. When people don't understand things, Mr. Martin pointed out, they tend to be afraid of them. The incident of the little girl the previous year was a good example. Although it had been shown that the so-called attack had never taken place, people still spoke of it as if it had actually happened.

"That's where you and Jenny can really help," he added quietly. "The people in the community need to know more about Apple Hill Farm, and the best way for people to get to know about things is through their kids."

It was this suggestion that Jenny and Billy were discussing as they climbed the hillside in back of Mrs. Ingersoll's apple orchard. The day before they had barely known about Apple Hill Farm, and now suddenly they found themselves designated as missionaries. In a way they were flattered, but they were also skeptical. Why would anyone listen to them?

"I think we should just see how it goes," Billy said finally. "If we like it, we can say so, and maybe some of the other kids will check it out."

"Think we should talk to Sol and some of the others about being counselors?"

"Let's wait and see." Billy stopped to catch his breath, leaning down to pet Skipper. Then he looked up the slope ahead of them. "It's getting pretty steep," he noted.

"It is."

Jenny and Billy had been planning to climb Dover Mountain for over a month. Actually Dover Mountain was not a single peak, but rather a long, high plateau that ran north of Paxton Road for almost five miles; a rugged, rocky terrain that had once been partially tamed, but that had now gone back to wilderness. It was twenty minutes before Jenny and Billy reached the final grade, and here they were stopped momentarily by a steep cliff twelve feet high. Billy tried to climb it, but soon gave up, and they began to circle in a northeasterly direction, looking for the old road Wes had mentioned to Billy.

"It's funny they'd build a road leading up here," Billy commented. "It must not have been easy."

"It probably wasn't, but they had to have one. People lived up here and mined iron for a long time. They were still mining it after the Revolutionary War, almost to the War of 1812. Mr. Farber told us in history class that they used iron from here to make cannon balls. They'd ship the iron down the Greene River on barges, and when they couldn't do that, because the English controlled the mouth of the river, they carried it over to the Hudson on wagons."

"How early did they start living up here?"

"We should be able to tell from the dates on the gravestones, if we can find the graveyard."

"We'll find it. It's just a little way from the deserted village. Drew said that the old stone house where they found Quarry is right next to it. Here's the road."

Jenny looked to where Billy was pointing. A rockslide of long ago had made a break in the cliff face, and the road climbed it on a diagonal. They scrambled up quickly, and then turned at the top to look back over the valley. In the distance, curving toward them, was the line of hills that separated Dover Valley from the Greene River Valley and below them was mile after mile of rich, rolling farmland, just beginning to take on color after the first frost.

"Think we should follow the old road?" Jenny asked, pointing to the double line of stone walls that led northeast from the top of the cut.

"Might as well. Better call Skipper."

Skipper had circled off to the left and was exploring a thicket of brambles. Jenny called him, and she and Billy started off. They walked carefully. Although it was late in the year for snakes, they were aware of Dover Mountain's reputation for harboring rattlesnakes and copperheads. Jenny was surprised that the stone walls to either side were still in such good condition, and she remarked on it as they walked along, speculating on whether the deserted village would be as well preserved.

"It isn't," Billy told her. "The houses were built of wood. All that's left are the foundations."

"Probably full of snakes."

"You're right. Sol Feldstein told me he saw four of them when he hiked up with his father last summer."

"How did they get up here?"

"They took the old road on the other side near the Dover Reservoir. It hooks up with this road a little way past the village."

They had been following the road for some time now, and it was gradually climbing. Although there was an occasional hemlock, most of the trees were oaks and maples with white birch clustered in small groves; slender, winter-bent trunks arching up toward the sun. The road itself was easy to follow since there was little underbrush, but Jenny and Billy were beginning to feel the effects of their long climb, and they were both relieved when they saw a tall stand of hemlocks just ahead. It looked cool, and they suspected the graveyard might lie beneath it.

"Where's Skipper?" Billy asked as they struggled up a final sharp rise in the road.

Jenny looked over her shoulder. "I don't know. I thought he was just behind us. He's probably hunting."

Resuming their climb, they soon reached the stand of hemlocks, and as they had hoped, they found the graveyard nestled at the foot of the trees. It was surrounded by a stone wall, and just back from the road fifteen yards short of the lower corner was a small stone house.

"Want to look at the house first or the graveyard?"

"Let's look at the graveyard."

Leading the way, Jenny walked quickly to the gap in the stone wall and stepped through. The graveyard was small. There were twenty-eight headstones in all. Jenny was surprised that it was not overgrown, but then she remembered that Wes Garavoy had told Billy he cut back the brush periodically. Walking to the far end,

Jenny bent down to study the corner headstone and gasped as she read the dates.

"Look at this!" she called. "1732 to 1770." This woman died before the Revolution!"

"This one's even older," Billy called back, peering at a stone further down the row. "This man died in 1737. He was born in Scotland."

Jenny started to walk toward him, but she stopped abruptly and stared at a long, flat stone lying on the ground at her feet.

"Billy, come here!"

"What?"

"Guess who's buried here? Jeremiah Tooks. He must be the one the road's named for."

"Him or his son. When did he die?"

"1818."

"Let's see how early and how late they were burying people here," Billy suggested, and he and Jenny quickly began to check the rest of the graves. They found that Jeremiah Tooks had been the last one to be buried, and that the first burial had been in 1733.

"It's funny so few people are buried here," Jenny mused, looking down at the grave of Jeremiah Tooks. "Let's see, 1733 to 1818 is eighty-five years. You'd think more than twenty-eight people would have been buried."

"Probably nobody lived up here but the miners, and they moved back down to the valley when they were too old to work in the mine. Who would want to live up here if they didn't have to? It must have been a pretty hard life."

"I wonder if Jeremiah Tooks was a miner?"

"He probably owned the mine. That's why they named it Tooks Hill Road."

"Maybe."

"Let's go look at the house."

They walked quickly to the corner of the graveyard and stepped into the path that led to the house. They had almost reached it when Billy came to an abrupt halt.

"Look!" he said, pointing to a rounded garbage pit beside the path. "There's fresh garbage in there. Someone must be staying in the house."

"How do you know it's fresh?"

"See for yourself."

Jenny stepped over to the edge of the hole and looked in. It was approximately three feet wide and four feet deep, and she could see that it had been in recent use for burning garbage. On the far side was a bag that had not yet been burned, and from the dryness of the paper, she guessed it had been tossed in that morning. She looked toward the house. Then she turned back to Billy who was watching her closely.

"Think we should go back?" he asked.

"Let's see if anybody's around first. Heck, we have as much right to be here as anyone else."

"What if it's Kurt Heineken, the guy Drew told us about?"

"What if it is?" Jenny stared at Billy who looked away, not meeting her glance. The truth was she had forgotten about Kurt Heineken until that moment. Now that Billy had reminded her, she was no more anxious to approach the house than he was, but she wasn't going to admit it. "Come on," she said firmly. "Let's have a look."

Leading the way, she walked rapidly along the path to the front door. Here she paused, listening for sounds from inside the house. She had almost decided to open the door, when Billy caught her elbow, whispering that someone was coming. At the same instant, Jenny, too, heard the sound of voices from the direction of the road. Motioning to Billy to follow, she ran to the corner of the house and crawled under a clump of mountain laurel, scrambling on all fours until she reached the center. Billy was right behind her.

"Hadn't we better go back further?" he asked in a whisper.

"They won't be able to see us," Jenny assured him. "Besides, I want to see who it is."

"You're crazy."

"If you want to go, go!"

"It's too late now."

The voices sounded very close, and seconds later two men stepped into view. The first was tall and lean with stooped shoulders and gray hair worn in a crew cut. His voice was harsh and low-pitched, and he walked with a slight limp. His companion was short and swarthy with thick black hair and a narrow, ferret-like face. Watching them, Jenny was very glad that she and Billy were well-hidden. The taller man had been speaking, but he fell silent as they walked to the door. They were both smoking, and the older man seemed preoccupied. Finally his companion rubbed out his cigarette and asked what they were going to do.

"What do you think we're going to do? We're going back to the old man."

"Why?"

"He was the last one to see Ed."

"What makes you so sure he knows something?"

"The money was here in this house. We've searched it from top to bottom, and there's no sign of anything. That means Ed must have moved it."

"So?"

"So he was hiding at the old man's place just before he was killed. He must have told him where he moved it."

"Old John was half nuts then, and he's three-quarter nuts now. He's probably forgotten about it."

"You don't know him. He's foxy. It would be just like him to sit on the money and laugh at the world."

"What makes you think he's going to tell *you* anything? He hates your guts."

"He'll talk. It may take time, but he'll talk. I've spent twelve years thinking about that money all day long every day, and no half-cracked old hermit is going to cheat me out of it now."

"He's a stubborn man."

"There's ways to make people talk; and after twelve years, I'm not going to worry overmuch about being nice."

"Why the hell did Ed ever bother with him?"

"He's Ed's uncle."

"Too bad you had the trouble with his son."

"It wasn't no trouble. He was out hunting and he was accidentally shot. Things happen that way."

"The old man's never seen it like that."

"So what? That's over a long time ago. Besides, I was Ed Quarry's friend." He was silent while he lighted a cigarette. "The way John puts away that muscatel, his tongue's going to get loose sooner or later. When it does, we pick up on it and start to apply the pressure."

"He'll laugh in your face."

The tall man had been looking toward the graveyard. He turned now and stared fixedly at his companion. "Look, little cousin, I don't have to take nothing off of you. You're either in this with me all the way, or you can get off the train right now. And I'll tell you something. I don't give a damn which you do."

"You came to me. I didn't come to you."

"Sure I came to you. But that's past." The older man stared at his companion, and abruptly he smiled. "Look, just in case you're getting any ideas about taking that money for yourself, forget them. You wouldn't last long against me. I just might have to break your back, and I wouldn't like to have to do that, seeing as you're family. No, little cousin, if I were you, I'd either do as I'm told, or I'd bail out now, and if you bail out, you'd better keep your mouth shut tight. You understand?"

The other nodded, and both were silent. Jenny was already looking behind her for a way to crawl further back, when the stillness was shattered by the sound of excited barking. It was Skipper, and it appeared that he was on the far side of the graveyard coming their way. Jenny glanced at the men. They had heard the barking and were standing tensely watching. Abruptly the older man said something in a low voice, and the two of them hurried off, skirting the near end of the graveyard and slipping into the bushes across the road. As the men disappeared from view, Billy touched Jenny on the arm and pointed toward the house. Jenny understood, and the two of them crawled rapidly through the bushes, keeping under cover until they were behind the house and could safely get to their feet.

"Keep the house between us and the men," Billy whispered. "We can join the road further down."

"What about Skipper?"

"He'll catch up to us."

Moving as quickly and silently as possible, they hurried away from the house. It was rough going, and for the first hundred yards or so, they didn't dare slow down. Only when the house was far behind them did they slow to a walk, but even then they moved rapidly, stopping only when they came to the road. Jenny settled on a flat stone atop the fence that bordered the road, while Billy sat on a stump to her right.

"Do you think that was Heineken?" Billy asked.

"Who else could it have been?"

"I guess you're right. It's funny. Yesterday Drew told us about Heineken, and today we saw him. It's almost like it was meant to happen. Do you think we should tell Captain Wiley?"

"I don't know. I don't want to get Debbie and Drew in trouble, and they're not supposed to have told us."

"Maybe we could tell Debbie, and she could tell her father. He's got to be told."

"Think we should tell him everything?"

Billy looked up puzzled. "What do you mean?"

"Maybe we could find out more, and then tell him."

"How?"

"Why don't we talk to the Garavoys?"

Jenny smiled as she observed her brother's startled expression. Actually the idea had occurred to her as they were watching Heineken and his cousin. It would be interesting to see how the Garavoys reacted to the news that Kurt Heineken was in the area and was looking for the money.

"That might not be too sharp," Billy said doubtfully.

"I don't see why not. Hey, here's Skipper."

Skipper was trotting toward them, his tongue hanging out and his tail waving excitedly. When he reached them, he came to a halt, ears cocked and tail barely stirring. Jenny reached down and petted him, running her hands along his coat and up his bushy tail to the tip. She glanced at Billy.

"What do you say? Do we go to the Garavoys?"

Billy shrugged. "It's your choice."

"Then I say we go. Come on."

They set off with Jenny in the lead, Billy a step behind, and Skipper bringing up the rear.

4 The Garavoys

HALF an hour later Jenny and Billy stepped into the Garavoy driveway. Seeing no sign of the brothers, they circled to the rear and knocked at the kitchen door. Lee, the younger brother, opened the door to let them in, pushing Skipper away with his foot when the dog tried to follow.

At first, coming from the bright sunlight into the interior darkness, they could see nothing. Then, as their eyes adjusted, they made out the tall, hulking figure of Wes Garavoy sprawled in a basket chair on the far side of the room.

"Have a seat, kids," he said softly. "Lee's got some cider if you're thirsty. Want some?"

They both nodded, and Lee picked up a gallon jug

from the counter and poured three glasses, taking one himself.

"So what's new?" Wes asked, once they were settled. "Any new plots against Lee and me?"

"Nothing I've heard," Billy replied. "Did Mr. Crabtree write you back?"

"Hell no! I told him I didn't want no answer, and if *he* wanted an answer, all he had to do was to step on my property and he'd get his answer in the seat of his pants!"

"Dad says he's got a lot of influence."

"He can go to hell. We're not selling, and that's that. Right, Lee?"

Lee made no response. He was staring fixedly at his two folded hands, and to look at him, one would have thought that he was paying no attention, but Jenny and Billy knew from experience that he was not missing a word.

"Dad says Crabtree is the one who's been trying to get the property away from the people at Apple Hill Farm," Jenny commented. "He's formed a landowners' association."

Wes let out a laugh that was half-grunt, half-exclamation. Getting to his feet, he walked over to refill his glass. Then he returned to his chair and sat down.

"He would do that. He's a meddler; can't stand to leave people alone. He's been in Dover Valley close to twenty-five years, and he's never stopped meddling.

Been buying property, too. This piece here, that piece there . . . Don't know what he figures to do with it. Been after Lee and me to sell, but we won't do it. No way. Condemn this property! I tell you, I'd like to see him try."

"Are they talking about condemning you?" Jenny asked, surprised.

"That's right. I showed Billy the letter. Crabtree's giving us this song and dance about straightening Paxton Road. He's got some state architect's plan to bypass the "S" curve by putting the road through our property. Prissy as hell! *Sincerely yours* . . . He doesn't have a sincere bone in his body."

"His letter said it would come up at the next town meeting," Lee noted softly. "Know when that is?"

"I think it's the end of October or early November," Jenny told him.

"Maybe we ought to go."

Lee glanced at Wes, but Wes shook his head slightly, and Lee did not pursue it.

"What have you two been up to all day?" Wes asked presently.

"We've been up on the mountain," Billy replied.

"You go to the graveyard?"

"Yes." Billy hesitated, glancing quickly at Jenny. She nodded, and he turned back to Wes. "We saw someone there."

"Someone?" Wes repeated softly. He was sipping his

cider, his hands interlocked around the glass, enveloping it.

"Two men. We think one of them was Kurt Heineken."

"Kurt Heineken!" Lee looked up abruptly, staring at Billy. "You couldn't have seen Kurt Heineken. He's in jail."

"He was paroled," Wes informed his brother. "Got out last week."

"Why the hell didn't you tell me?"

"I only just heard." Wes turned to Billy. "The guy with Heineken. Was he short and heavyset, black hair?"

Billy nodded.

"Cousin Greg; it figures. So they're up in the old caretaker's house? I thought they'd be around sooner or later."

"Who's Cousin Greg?" Billy asked.

"He's Heineken's first cousin. Lots of muscle, but not much brain."

"He seemed scared of Heineken."

"I expect he is. Most people are. I've never known anyone who wasn't, except maybe Ed Quarry."

"You knew him?"

"We all did. Dover Valley's not that big."

"Shut up, Wes."

Wes glanced at his brother, then settled back in his chair with his eyes half-closed. Two flies had settled on the table in front of Lee, attracted by some spilled sugar. He watched them, raising his hand slowly. Suddenly he slapped it down, shaking the table, but the flies were too quick for him and flew away. He swore softly and, getting to his feet, walked out of the room. Moments later they heard the front door slam shut.

"What's wrong with him?" Billy asked.

"There's bad blood between him and Heineken. That's why I ain't said nothing."

"Sorry."

" 'Tain't your fault. He would have found out sooner or later." He shook his head, frowning down at his glass. "I should've known it would come to this."

"What do you mean?"

"Did you just see them, or did you hear them talking?"

"We heard them talking," Jenny told him. "They were talking about an old man and about some money. Heineken said that the money had been in the house, and since it wasn't there anymore, Ed Quarry must have moved it. Heineken thinks the old man must know where it's hidden. He said they'd just have to keep after him. From what he was saying, it sounded like the old man was Quarry's uncle. Do you know him?"

"Yeah, I know John Quarry. Heineken's not going to get anything out of him. He hates Heineken's guts."

"They said that. Why?"

"Old John's son was killed in a hunting accident.

He and Heineken had had a falling out. It was just before Heineken was arrested. There was a lot of talk, but nobody could prove nothing."

"If Heineken knows that, how come he thinks the old man will tell him?"

"Probably thinks he can force it out of him, and maybe he can. He can be mean when he sets about it."

"Think we ought to warn the old man?" Billy asked.

"He knows the score."

"Maybe he could use some help. Maybe we ought to tell Captain Wiley what we heard."

Wes stood up and crossed the kitchen to pour himself another glass of cider. He sipped it slowly, looking out the window. Finally he turned back to face them.

"I'll tell you about Ed Quarry. After the shoot-out, Ed moved around a lot to keep one step ahead of the law. He even stayed with us a few days." Wes paused, as if daring them to comment, but Jenny and Billy remained silent. "The thing is, we were all born and raised around here, and we all knew Ed. He helped a lot of people. Sure, he and his gang robbed houses, but it was from people who had plenty. Mind you, I'm not holding no brief for him and the others. What they did was wrong. Only we didn't want to be the ones to do the turning-in. People liked Ed. Heineken's another story. People wouldn't have helped Heineken the way they did Ed. Ed stayed a lot of different places, and the police knew it, only they couldn't catch him. It was something every one of us was in together. If the police had wanted to make something of it, they'd have had to have arrested half the people between here and Hungerford."

He finished his cider and put the glass in the sink, returning to his chair and sitting down. Jenny and Billy remained where they were.

"The two places Ed stayed most often were over at Apple Hill Farm and up on the mountain. Apple Hill was deserted then, and Ed spent many a night there. Then he almost got caught one night, and he never went back. Up on the mountain he used to stay with his uncle, John Quarry, when he wasn't staying in the stone house by the graveyard. You'd think the police would have watched John Quarry's house, but the reason they didn't is there was a feud between Old John and Ed's father, and nobody knew that Ed and Old John had made it up. The police did check both places now and then, but Ed always got out of sight until they were gone."

"How come the police knew where to go the day they found him?"

"They were tipped off," Wes replied, glancing quickly at Billy, who had asked the question. "How did you know about it?"

"Drew Wiley told us. He says they found him with a gun in his hand. They think he shot himself."

"So they're still trying to pretend it was a suicide." Wes fell silent, shaking his head in disgust.

"What do *you* think?" Jenny asked.

Wes turned to Jenny, and abruptly he smiled. "You really want to know? Ed didn't shoot himself. He was shot. And Wiley damn well knows it! Ed would no more shoot himself than I'd lick Gene Crabtree's boot. Besides, I saw him."

"Who?"

"Ed Quarry. I needed a loan, and he was going to give it to me. He did that a lot, helping to tide people over. He knew his life wasn't worth a plugged nickel if the people turned against him. That's why he did favors. Heineken and the others thought he was nuts, but it paid off for him, at least for a while. The other guys in the gang were like Heineken. Ed, he was the brains; he was the smart one."

"When did you see him?"

"The morning of the day he was killed. Lee and I climbed up to the stone house real early, but Ed was already up and around. He seemed like he was in a big hurry. He told us he had to meet someone; that he'd be going away. He gave us the money and told us to pay it back to Old John. Then he asked Lee if he had a good pair of boots he could have. Him and Lee wore the same size. As it happened, Lee did have an extra pair, and Ed asked him to bring them up later. When we came back, we found him shot."

"Did you tell the police?" Jenny asked.

"Nope. I learned long ago to keep my mouth shut when it comes to things like that. That way Lee and I stay out of trouble. We figured we'd let the police know indirectly, but someone beat us to it."

"Did Ed Quarry say whom he was going to meet?" Billy asked.

"No, and I don't even have a guess." He paused, watching them closely. "The reason I'm telling you this is that with Heineken out, the pot just might start to simmer again. I'd as soon the old man didn't get hurt. He's a crazy old coot, but I like him. Someone got something out of killing Ed, and Heineken wants to find out what and who. I'd just as soon Wiley knows that, if he doesn't already, and knows where Ed was staying and what happened that last day."

"Why don't you tell him yourself?" Jenny asked.

"I'd rather he got it from you two. That way I haven't said anything official, if he ever decides to make anything of it."

"Do you think John Quarry knows who killed Ed?" Billy asked.

"I doubt it. He was over in Dixville the whole day."

"What's he like?"

"He was a hard man in his time, but he's mellowed. Knows the woods better than I do. He never had no formal schooling, but he knows more about this part of the country than all the schoolteachers put together. He can tell you how people used to live around here when they were mining iron ore on Dover Mountain. He's got a collection of Indian tools, and he must have every tool the early colonists ever used." He paused, regarding them thoughtfully. "Maybe I'll take you with me when I go up there. Might loosen the old boy up. You'd learn a thing or two."

"Sure he wouldn't mind?"

"He might, but once you told him just what you told me, he'd be too busy thinking. And by the way, when you're talking to Captain Wiley, don't say anything about the loan. Just say we saw Ed that morning, and tell him about the boots. That kinda proves the point. Why get a pair of new boots if he was thinking of suicide that same day? And another thing. I wouldn't mention about going to see John. That'll be our secret for now."

"When do you want to go?" Billy asked.

"Sometime this week. I'll let you know." He turned his head as he heard the front door slam. "Don't say nothing to Lee," he cautioned.

They nodded, and a moment later Lee stepped into the room. Seeing Billy and Jenny still seated at the table, he glanced at Wes, eyebrows raised in inquiry.

"Billy and Jenny are just leaving," Wes observed placidly. "Where you been?"

"Walkin'," Lee answered, sitting down at the kitchen table. His eyes settled on Jenny, as she and Billy got to their feet preparatory to leaving. "Your dog's outside."

Jenny thanked him, and she and Billy moved to the door. As they were walking away, they heard a loud thump, followed by a muttered curse. Lee had taken another swipe at the flies on the kitchen table and had missed again.

"Why do you think Wes wants to take us when he goes to see John Quarry?" Billy asked as soon as they were out of earshot.

"I don't know," Jenny replied cautiously. "What do you think?"

"Maybe he thinks Old John knows where Quarry hid the money."

"So?"

"When we tell him what Heineken said, he may tell us something."

"Why should he?"

"Why else would Wes take us?"

"I don't know." Jenny glanced at her brother, but Billy's eyes were on the pavement. It was a puzzle.

5 Captain Wiley

After leaving the Garavoys, Jenny and Billy went directly to the Wiley house. Seeing no sign of Debbie and Drew in the yard, they knocked on the front door. To their surprise, it was Captain Wiley himself who opened it.

"What can I do for you two?" he asked, squatting down to pet Skipper, who was sniffing his trousers. "Drew and Debbie hiked into the village. I don't expect them back for an hour."

"Well, actually we came to talk to you," Jenny explained somewhat hesitantly. "We think we saw Kurt Heineken on the mountain."

"Heineken!" Captain Wiley stood up quickly, his eyes on Jenny. "How do you know about him?"

"Everybody knows about him. He was part of the Quarry gang."

"So he was." Captain Wiley watched them closely, then turned, holding the door open. "Come into the office."

"So you think you saw Kurt Heineken?" he asked when they had settled into chairs opposite his desk.

They both nodded.

"Tell me about it."

Jenny glanced at Billy, and catching his nod, she launched into the story, describing much of the conversation between Heineken and his cousin. Then she told about Wes Garavoy having seen Ed Quarry the morning of the murder, and his belief that Quarry's death had not been a suicide. Captain Wiley listened without comment, although his eyebrows did shoot up when the Garavoys were mentioned. When Jenny had finished, he remained silent for some time. Then abruptly he stood up and stepped across to a bookcase. Taking a pile of photographs from a manilla folder, he handed them to Jenny and Billy, asking if they recognized any of the men pictured. They studied the photographs carefully, finally selecting two of them. Captain Wiley glanced at the ones they had selected and smiled.

"Well, you seem to have seen Heineken and his cousin all right."

He paused thoughtfully, scratching the back of his neck. "Did Wes Garavoy suggest that you come to me?"

"It was our idea," Jenny replied, "but he agreed with it."

"How do you happen to know Wes?"

"Billy met him first," Jenny said, and Billy went on to explain about Wes cutting himself, and how he had helped him.

Captain Wiley nodded and stretched back in his chair, staring up at the ceiling. He had taken a cigar from his shirt pocket and was rolling it back and forth in his hand. Finally he put it in his mouth and lit it.

"Did Wes say why he waited until now to speak up?"

Jenny looked at Billy, and it was Billy who answered. "He was worried about John Quarry. He said he thought you should know what Heineken had said, and why Heineken would think John Quarry might know about the money."

Captain Wiley laughed. "He's got a point."

"He wanted you to know about Ed Quarry, too," Jenny added. "Quarry was planning to go away. Why would he have asked Lee to bring him a pair of boots if he were planning to kill himself?"

Captain Wiley glanced at her, but said nothing. He smoked in silence, leaning well back in his chair. Then abruptly he seemed to reach a decision. "Can you two keep a secret?"

They nodded.

"Wes Garavoy is one hundred percent correct when he says it wasn't a suicide. It was set up to look that way, but it was murder. There's not a shadow of doubt about that."

"Have you ever gotten back any of the money?" Billy asked.

"Not a cent. That's why we pretended to believe it was suicide. We hoped it would make the murderer careless. No, the Quarry murder is one of those crimes we've never been able to solve. We questioned John Quarry, of course, but he had an air-tight alibi. He had been in Dixville all day. There was nobody else, and when the money didn't turn up, it left us with nothing to go on."

"What are you going to do about Heineken?"

"Not much. He's served his time. As long as he keeps his nose clean and doesn't violate the terms of his parole, there's nothing we can do. Of course, we can keep an eye on him, and it helps to know that he's up on Dover Mountain. We may pull him in for questioning, just so he knows we're watching him, but I may not even do that. I'd as soon give him his head. He's the type of lightning rod that usually draws lightning, and we may find out something."

He picked up a sheet of paper from his desk and studied it. Then he put it down and leaned forward to deposit his cigar ash in the big glass ashtray on the far side of his desk, his eyes falling on Jenny as he did so.

"By the way, you say Wes and Lee were both up on the mountain on the day of the murder?"

"That's what Wes said."

"Did he tell you why?"

"No. He just told us about seeing Ed Quarry and about his wanting to borrow a pair of Lee's boots."

Captain Wiley nodded, tapping his fingers gently on the edge of the desk. He sat motionless for some time. The room was very quiet, and Jenny and Billy began to shift uneasily on their chairs. Finally Captain Wiley stood up. Thanking them for coming and complimenting them on the way in which they had handled themselves, he led the way to the front door. As they were about to leave, he cautioned them to say nothing about Heineken or about the circumstances of Ed Quarry's death.

"The less talk there is, the better. And if I were you," he added, "I'd stay away from Dover Mountain."

"Should we say anything to Wes Garavoy?" Billy asked.

"Just tell him you talked to me."

Giving them a parting wave, he stepped back inside and closed the door.

"Do you think he suspects the Garavoys?" Jenny asked as they were walking away.

"No telling. All I know is we did what Wes said."

Jenny nodded, and for the next few yards they walked in silence.

"How well do you know Lee?" Jenny asked suddenly.

"Not as well as I know Wes. Lee never talks much.

He lets Wes do the talking. Sometimes he puts in a question, like when he asked about the town meeting. He gets mad sometimes, too. I don't think Lee really likes anybody, except maybe Wes, and I'm not always sure he likes him. Why?"

"Why do you think Lee went out of the house when he did?"

"I don't know. That's just the way he acts."

"Do you think Wes is protecting him?"

"It could be, only it doesn't make sense. If he were protecting him, why tell us about the two of them being on the mountain the day Ed Quarry was murdered? He didn't have to tell us."

Jenny nodded, and nothing more was said until they were about to turn into their own driveway. Then Jenny suggested that they stop by the Garavoys on their way back from Apple Hill Farm the next day.

"What if Lee's there?" Billy asked.

"Maybe you can ask Wes to show you something."

Billy thought about it. "Okay. Hey, there's Skipper."

Sure enough Skipper was waiting for them on the back porch. He had run off when they had gone inside to speak with Captain Wiley, and they hadn't seen him since. As usual, he greeted them enthusiastically, and they were a cheerful threesome as they stepped through the back door.

6 First Day at Apple Hill

WHEN Jenny and Billy climbed off the school bus with Diane Drake and the two Wileys next afternoon, they were both apprehensive. It had been one thing to talk about working with the campers, but now that they were there, they wondered whether they would really be able to do the job or would just be in the way. Diane tried to reassure them, but they only half-listened. They walked up the drive quickly and turned into the path that led to the Drake house. Evidently Mr. Drake had been watching for them, because he was waiting outside the kitchen door with two of the campers beside him. After speaking briefly to Diane, he introduced the Martins and the Wileys to the two campers, explaining that they would guide them to their work areas and introduce them to the counselors in charge.

"Usually I'd take you around," he added, "but I have a meeting of the trustees in five minutes. I'll see you after you finish, though, and I'll try to introduce you to Larry Carrington, our Director." He turned to Diane. "Do you want to work with Jenny today, Di?"

Diane glanced at Jenny and winked. "Okay with me, unless you want me to talk to the trustees."

Mr. Drake laughed. "I think you can leave that to me."

They chatted a moment more, and then a large station wagon drove up to the main office and Mr. Drake hurried away. As soon as he had gone, Diane turned to the older of the two campers.

"Are you going to take Billy and Drew to the woodworking shop, George?"

George glanced quickly at his fellow camper, a tall, blonde girl named Polly. He seemed perplexed, and it was a moment before he answered.

"Ralph isn't there," he announced finally. "Should we go look for him?"

"He probably had to go to the meeting. Why don't you wait in the shop for him? You can show Billy and Drew what you're working on."

George smiled shyly and nodded. Glancing at the boys to make sure that they had heard, he started toward the long, low-roofed shed, which housed the woodworking shop. Billy and Drew followed him, and the three soon disappeared through a doorway at the far end of the building.

"We'd better make tracks to the sewing room," Diane said. "We'll drop you at the ceramics shed on the way, Debbie."

Turning to her right, Diane started off rapidly, and the others fell into step behind her. On the way Jenny sneaked several quick glances at Polly. She guessed that the girl was in her late teens. She was tall, with long blonde hair, and her face was quite pretty, although marred by the slackness of feature Jenny had noticed in many of the campers.

"Here's the pottery shed," Diane announced. "You two wait here while I take Debbie inside and introduce her to Mrs. Carrington."

"Is she the wife of the director?" Debbie asked.

"Right. She's been in charge of ceramics ever since we started."

Moments later Diane reappeared, and they continued on their way to the sewing room. When they reached it, Diane stepped inside and deposited her schoolbooks on a table near the door, indicating to Jenny that she should do likewise. Then they walked up the room past the knitters and needlepointers until they reached a cluster of three tables at the far end. A woman was already sitting there with two campers, and Diane quickly introduced Jenny. The woman, Mrs. Smart, greeted her warmly, and the two campers, both girls of about Polly's age, smiled and nodded. The shorter of the two, a pudgy-faced brunette with closely-cropped hair, patted the seat next to her, and after glancing at Diane to be sure she was doing the correct thing, Jenny sat there. Polly promptly took the seat on Jenny's right, while Diane sat next to the other camper on Mrs. Smart's left.

As soon as Jenny was seated, the pudgy-faced girl, whose name was Phyllis, handed her a Raggedy Ann doll. She was obviously proud of it, and Jenny looked it over admiringly, noting the meticulous stitching on the body of the doll itself and on the clothes in which it was dressed.

"Phyllis did all the work on that one," Mrs. Smart explained. "She sewed it and stuffed it and fitted the clothes to it. It will make some little girl very happy, don't you think, Phyl?"

Phyllis nodded, smiling shyly at Jenny.

"Up to now we've done mostly Raggedy Ann dolls and stuffed animals. Phyl has quite a collection, don't you, Phyl?"

The girl nodded again, blinking with embarrassment and giggling.

"Look at this dog, Jenny," Diane said, passing a stuffed dog by way of Mrs. Smart. "Carrie made this. Are you going to keep it and give it a name, Carrie, or are you going to let us sell it?"

Carrie, a dark-haired girl with shiny black eyes, glanced quickly at Mrs. Smart, and then at Jenny. She was silent for several seconds, evidently weighing Diane's question.

"I think we could sell it. I already have a gray dog."

Mrs. Smart laughed, ruffling Carrie's hair. "I think that's a good decision, Carrie. We need some dogs for the next shipment. Do you feel like doing another?"

Again Carrie paused to consider. Then she nodded, speaking very slowly in a firm, controlled voice. "I think I'll make a brown one this time, and I'll put a longer tail on him. Children like long tails. They can pull them."

"Good. A brown dog it will be. Better pick out your material."

While Carrie scrambled out of her chair and walked over to the two large boxes of vari-colored cloth remnants, Mrs. Smart talked with Phyllis and Polly about their projects. Then she turned to Diane.

"Diane, could you stay with the girls while I show Jenny what we make?"

Diane had already started to cut out cloth for Phyllis, and she nodded without looking up from what she was doing. Getting to her feet, Jenny followed Mrs. Smart down the room to the far end where there were several rows of shelves crammed with dolls, knitted goods, leather work, and other handicrafts.

"This is where we assemble all the things the children make," Mrs. Smart explained. "When we have enough for a shipment, we pack them in boxes, and

Mr. Carrington takes them down to New York City to our sales outlet."

"Don't you sell some of them here?" Jenny asked.

"We sell a few things here, especially to the parents and friends who come to visit, but most of our things go either to New York or to Boston." She laughed abruptly, indicating the well-filled shelves with a gesture. "You see, we make too much. We'd never be able to sell it all locally. We have almost enough for a shipment now, and this is only three weeks' work."

"Do the campers keep many of the things they make?"

"A few. We'd better get back to work now."

The rest of the afternoon passed rapidly. Polly, Jenny discovered, was extremely competent and needed little help, but Carrie and Phyllis required frequent advice and constant encouragement. Mrs. Smart remained silent, leaving it to Diane and Jenny to shoulder the instructional burden and observing how they handled it. At the end of the afternoon, as they were putting the materials away, she took Diane and Jenny aside and complimented them on how well they had done.

"I think you two make a good team," she observed, watching the three campers who were dusting the table and sweeping the floor. "Do you think you could handle the three girls if I were to start up another group?"

Jenny glanced at Diane, but Diane had her eyes on Mrs. Smart. "I'd have to ask Mom and Dad," she said finally. "I'd like to work with Jenny, but they think I should get into more activities at school."

"Do you think you could work three afternoons a week?"

"Maybe."

"I'd like to get more of the campers into sewing. If we could manage two groups of six between us, I think we could really get something going. What do you think, Jenny?"

"I think we could. In fact, if Diane can do two afternoons with me, I expect I can manage the third alone. Polly's pretty good, and I'm sure she could help me."

Mrs. Smart agreed. "I think she could. Actually, Polly could go home now, but she's happy here, and her family seems to prefer that she stay."

"Don't they want her home?"

Mrs. Smart hesitated before answering, her eyes on Polly. "I don't think so," she said finally. "Her father was killed in Korea, and her mother is remarried and has a new family. It's one of those things."

For a moment they were silent. Then the three campers came up to them, and they all walked to the door where Diane and Jenny picked up their schoolbooks. As they emerged into the late afternoon sunlight, a bell rang several times, and when Jenny asked about it, Diane explained that it was a signal for the kitchen crew to report to work.

"What do you do if you're not on kitchen crew?" Jenny asked Polly, who was walking beside her.

"Anything we want. I'm going to write my mother. She lives out in California where I used to live."

A few minutes later they reached the dining hall and recreation area, and the three campers left after being assured that Jenny and Diane would be working with them again on Wednesday.

"Where's Billy?" Jenny asked.

"He and Drew are probably at my house," Diane replied. "Dad said for me to bring you over after we finished."

"I'll go with you then," Mrs. Smart said. "I imagine Ralph is there, and we can walk back to the house together. Ralph's my husband," she added for Jenny's benefit. "He's in charge of the woodworking shop."

When they reached the Drake house, they found not only Billy, Drew, and Mr. Smart, but Mr. and Mrs. Carrington and Debbie as well.

"Well, how did it go?" Mr. Carrington asked as they stepped into the kitchen.

"I think you've got a good team here," Mrs. Smart replied. "In fact, I'm hoping they'll take over sewing group one so I can start a new group."

"What do you girls think of that?"

Jenny started to speak, but held back, her eyes on Diane, who was watching her mother. Mrs. Drake turned to her husband. "Tom?"

Mr. Drake looked back at her, then turned to Diane. "Di, I think it's up to you." He glanced at Mrs. Smart. "It would be three afternoons a week, right, Nora?"

Mrs. Smart nodded.

"Well, what do you think, Di?"

"I want to, and Jenny does, too."

"I guess that does it. You've got your team, Nora. And Ralph's got a team coming along, too. Billy and Drew."

"Well done." Mr. Carrington glanced around the circle, obviously pleased with the day's accomplishments. "Now if we can get old Crabtree off our necks and raise a little money, we'll really have something to celebrate."

"Is he up to anything new?" Mrs. Smart asked in alarm.

"Same old thing. He's been in touch with the trustees. He's raised the offer, and he's pushing them to push us. He's also trying to get the state health examiner in here."

"He already did that," Mr. Drake muttered angrily. "We passed."

"He's got a new wrinkle, something about the size of our sewage plant. He's told the trustees we'll be in for some surprises at the next town meeting."

"That could be trouble."

"I know it." Mr. Carrington frowned. Then he seemed to shake it off and looked up with a smile. "We'll just have to outlast him. That's all there is to it. Give the man enough rope and he'll hang himself."

"He may hang us first."

Mr. Carrington glanced at Mr. Drake. "I don't think so, Tom. If we keep on the way we're going, sentiment is bound to shift in our favor. I think today is a good beginning."

"I hope you're right."

"I am." Mr. Carrington fell silent, his eyes on the floor. Then he turned to Debbie. "By the way, Debbie, your mother called to say that she'd be picking up you and Drew on her way back from Greene River."

"Did she say when?"

"Should be any time now."

After that the conversation became general. Jenny and Billy talked briefly to Diane and her mother. Then Billy asked Jenny in a whisper whether she still wanted to stop by the Garavoys on their way home.

"Sure."

"Let's go then."

They left a few minutes later and walked quickly down the driveway. Turning left on Paxton Road, they set off at a good clip. They soon reached the Garavoy house, but there a surprise awaited them. Parked in the driveway was a police car.

"Think it's Captain Wiley?" Jenny asked.

"Probably. Wes will be griped."

"Why? We didn't tell Captain Wiley anything he said not to tell him. He knew we were going to talk to him."

"I hope you're right." Billy studied the house, then glanced at his sister. "We can stop tomorrow after school."

"Okay with me."

Turning, Billy walked away, and Jenny fell into step beside him. It was nearly sundown, and shadows already covered most of the road. As they turned into their own driveway, a car drove up behind them and pulled to a stop. It was Captain Wiley.

"You two been wandering on the mountain again?" he asked with a grin.

Jenny shook her head. "We're working at Apple Hill Farm."

Captain Wiley nodded. "Debbie told me about that." He paused, and Jenny sensed that he was watching them. "I had a talk with Wes Garavoy."

"Was Lee there?" Billy asked.

"No. He was helping Neil Bishop unload some freight." Captain Wiley tapped his cigar on the window ledge, and the flare of the ash lighted his face momentarily. Jenny thought that he looked tired; tired and a little worried. "I thought it was about time Wes and I laid some cards on the table. He told me he was thinking of going to see John Quarry and taking you two along. I think it's a good idea."

"Did he say when he intends to go?"

"No, but I'd keep in touch with him if I were you. You might drop by tomorrow."

"We were going to."

"Good."

"Why does Wes want to take us along?" Jenny asked.

"Unless I'm mistaken, it's because he knows Old John doesn't trust him. You see, people have been after that money for years, and if Wes were to go up there alone, Quarry might figure he was just trying to use Heineken to scare him into saying where the money is. On the other hand, if he brings you two, and the Old Man hears from you what you overheard, it might make more of an impression on him. That's what's important to Wes. He's got serious fish to fry, and he wants Old John to open up a bit about what happened after the shoot-out."

"Why?"

Captain Wiley was silent, and Jenny thought that he was not going to answer. Then abruptly he did.

"You're likely to find out sooner or later, so I might as well tell you now. In fact, it might be better if you know. Lee Garavoy was part of the gang until he had a run-in with Heineken and dropped out. Mind you, I can't prove that, but you can take my word that it's true. Later, when we went back into the hills after the gang, we didn't catch either Heineken or Ed Quarry. In fact, we didn't catch Heineken until a week later. Then we got a tip, and we trapped him. Heineken blamed it on Lee, and he swore that he'd get even sooner or later. I imagine Wes wants to get a line on who did turn in Heineken before Heineken comes after Lee."

"Don't you know who turned in Heineken?"

"No. There was a printed note stuck under my door; that's all. Wes didn't say so, but I believe he thinks it was Ed Quarry himself who turned in Heineken. If that's the case, he may be hoping he can persuade John Quarry to tell that to Heineken. Make sense?"

Jenny nodded. "Sort of."

"It would be a case of asking John to do him a favor in return for his favor in bringing you two. He figures that if Quarry did turn in Heineken, Old John knows about it."

"Do you think John Quarry will do what he wants?" Billy asked.

"Maybe, maybe not. What I want you to do is to go along with Wes and tell Old John what you overheard. When you get back, let me know, and I'll be in touch with you."

"What if we meet Heineken?"

"You won't. Heineken doesn't want to be seen. Besides, even if you meet him, there won't be any problem. He doesn't know you, and he has no reason to tangle with Wes. He wants that money, and that's the only thing he's interested in."

Jenny and Billy nodded, and giving them a parting wave, Captain Wiley started his engine and drove off.

"Think we should say something to Mom and Dad?" Billy asked as they walked back toward the steps.

"Not yet. Let's wait until after we go to see John Quarry."

Billy nodded. Jenny was usually right when it came to dealing with their parents.

7 John Quarry

When Jenny and Billy arrived at the Garavoys the next afternoon, they found Wes in the back yard chopping firewood. It was an unusually warm day, and Wes was shirtless. Seeing Jenny and Billy, he buried his axe in a log, and pulling a red bandanna from his back pocket, wiped the sweat off his face and neck.

"Hot enough, ain't it?" he observed as he stuffed the bandanna back into his pocket. "You two just out of school?"

Billy nodded.

"Where's your dog?"

"We left him home."

"Captain Wiley was up here last night."

"I know. We saw his car on our way back from Apple Hill."

"What were you doing there?"

"We're working there now."

Wes sat down on the stump he had been using as a chopping block.

"Apple Hill Farm, that's where they have those retarded people, ain't it?" Although he phrased it as a question, Jenny and Billy could tell that he didn't expect an answer. "Apple Hill's a good farm, rich land. I wouldn't mind owning a piece of property like that."

"Mr. Crabtree's trying to buy it," Jenny observed quietly.

"You told me before." Wes shook his head in disgust. "Man must be crazy. Doesn't use half his own land, and he's looking around to buy more. You ever seen him?"

Jenny shook her head.

"He's a funny-looking guy. Long scrawny neck like a chicken. Looks as if you could blow him over, but I guess he's got some bantam bred into him. Can't stomach him myself, and Lee can't neither, but he's got his points. He's a smart devil, and like I say, he's got guts in his own queer way. He came walking into the house yesterday, cool as a cucumber. That's why I say he's got guts; either that or he's just plain crazy!"

"He came over here?" Billy asked in surprise. "Why?"

"Wanted to know if we'd got his letter." Wes looked at Billy, and suddenly he burst out laughing. "Believe me, I told him."

"What did he say?"

"Well, first he asked about the letter. When I told him as how I wasn't moving for no road, he started to sound me out about Apple Hill, said there might be a vote coming up next town meeting. I think he had a deal in mind; Lee's and my votes on Apple Hill, and no more talk about road-straightening."

"What did you tell him?"

"I didn't tell him nothing. Said Lee and me would think about it. He said he'd talk to us again."

"Did he ask you not to say anything about it?"

Wes glanced at Jenny, and abruptly he grinned. "Now how did you guess that?"

"How are you going to vote?"

Wes was silent for a moment, his eyes on Jenny. "Figure it this way," he said finally. "Anything Crabtree's for, chances are Lee and I are against. That's the way the wind blows, particularly when anybody tries to push us. Only Crabtree don't know it. Heck, I don't know one thing or the other about Apple Hill Farm, and I care less, but if Gene Crabtree wants to put the whammy on it, then I'm all for it. And Lee, too."

"Where is Lee?"

"Over to Greene River. We needed some parts."

"Do you mind if I tell Mr. Carrington at Apple Hill

Farm what Mr. Crabtree said?" Jenny asked. "He's the director there."

"Tell anybody you like. Ain't no call for me to keep Gene Crabtree's secrets."

Wes began to roll a cigarette, holding the paper in his left hand while he shook the tobacco from a small sack.

"Feel like a walk?" he asked abruptly.

"Where to?"

"Thought we might climb up Dover Mountain and have a talk with John Quarry."

"Where does he live?"

"About half a mile past the village. He built himself a shack handy to the spring." Wes stretched and stood up, reaching for his shirt, which hung on a nearby branch. "Want to go?"

"Sure."

Five minutes later they had crossed the road and were climbing the easy grade through the wood lot. Wes was wearing his shirt now, and he was carrying a shotgun cradled under his arm. When Jenny asked about it, Wes laughed and said that he might pick up a squirrel or a rabbit on the way back. Reaching the upper boundary of the wood lot, they followed a stone wall until they came to a gap flanked by a grove of birch trees.

"If you're trying to find the trail another time, look for the birch trees," Wes told them. "You can see them from our mailbox."

"Do you think we're likely to run into Heineken?" Billy asked.

Wes shook his head. "Not the way I'm gonna take you. Come on. We'd better make tracks."

With Wes leading the way, they followed a twisting trail that joined the old road a few yards short of the cliff. Then they climbed up on the path that Jenny and Billy had used, but when they reached the top, instead of taking the old road, Wes turned to the northeast, following the line of the cliff until he came to a barely discernible trail that set off in a northerly direction.

"This was a wagon track back in the old days," Wes explained. "The deer have been using it for years, and Old John comes this way now and again when he needs supplies from Greene River."

"How does he get down the cliff?"

"He slides down; comes back up the other route." Wes chuckled suddenly, glancing at Billy over his shoulder. "Got me a nice buck here two years back. Only trouble was it was a week before season."

"What did you do with it?"

"Hung the carcass in the house by the graveyard. Stone house in the woods is a good place to hang meat," he added in explanation.

"How far do we have to go?" Jenny called from behind Billy.

"Couple of miles. We going too fast for you?"

"I'll keep up," Jenny replied grimly.

The trail was a rough one, and both she and Billy found it hard going. Wes strode on ahead, moving easily, and they both envied him his long legs and effortless surefootedness. Whereas they stumbled over rocks and half-buried roots and had their faces slashed repeatedly by unexpected branches, he seemed to avoid every hazard.

They had been walking for some time, and Jenny was beginning to wish they had brought a water bottle with them, when Wes came to an abrupt halt, holding up his hand to signal them to do likewise. Seconds later they heard the sound of voices in the distance, or rather the sound of a single, loud, angry voice. Although they listened carefully, neither Jenny nor Billy could make out what was being said. A second voice was even more indistinct. After a final burst from the louder voice, there was silence. Wes listened a while longer, then turned to Jenny and Billy.

"Seems as how John's got visitors," he said softly.

"Think it's Heineken and his cousin?" Billy asked.

"Most likely."

"Maybe we should go back."

"My daddy used to say a man gets the most by striking while the iron's hot."

"What if Heineken and his cousin come back?"

"We'll get a mite closer and give it time for the dust to settle. I expect Heineken's still there."

"How do you know?"

"No sound of his leaving. Keep quiet as you can."

They moved forward more slowly this time, stepping carefully so as to make as little noise as possible. Fifty yards further on they came to a grove of hemlocks, and here Wes stopped, motioning them closer.

"We're pretty near John's house now. Reason we could hear the voices before was we were downwind."

"Has Heineken left yet?"

"Don't think so. Let's sit tight and listen."

For fifteen minutes they waited. There had been no further sound of voices, and indeed only an occasional whiff of wood smoke suggested human habitation. It was very still. The only sounds were the persistent drone of the wind blowing through the tops of the hemlocks and the muted calls of birds in the undergrowth around them. Once, off in the distance, they heard the harsh calls of a flock of crows, but there was nothing else. In fact, it was so silent that when a twig snapped with a crack like a gunshot off to their left, it startled them.

"What's that?" Jenny whispered anxiously, but Wes shook his head, motioning her to be silent. He was listening closely, and she and Billy watched him uneasily, knowing that his keener senses were registering signs and sounds that they could not discern. Finally he got to his feet.

"They've gone now. Let's see what Old John has to say."

Leaving the hemlock grove, they passed through a mini-forest of birch before reaching a small brook, which tumbled down through the trees in a series of tiny waterfalls and leaf-dammed pools. They all stooped to drink and Wes explained that the brook originated in a spring behind John Quarry's shack. On the other side of the brook the growth thinned out, and the scent of woodsmoke permeated the air.

"The Old Man must be doing some burning," Wes remarked casually, but Jenny sensed a note of worry in his voice. Then they stepped into a sunlit clearing. Wes stopped, and Jenny and Billy stopped with him. Across the clearing was a low-lying cabin, and just to the right of it a burn barrel, topped by a cloud of thick gray smoke.

"Wet leaves," Wes observed. "I'm glad it's the burn barrel and not the house."

"Did you think they had set fire to the house?"

"I was hoping they hadn't."

"Stop right there!"

The voice had come from their right, and they turned in that direction. A man was standing at the edge of the trees, a shotgun in his hands. He was tall and powerfully built, with shoulder-length white hair and a full white beard that reached to his chest. He watched them in silence, not moving a muscle, and they, too, were silent. Perhaps it was a trick of the sunlight, but the old man's eyes seemed to flash as he surveyed them. Finally he slipped the shotgun into the crook of his arm.

"What brings you here, Wesley Garavoy?"

"I want to talk to you, John."

The old man stared at him. Finally he nodded, and crossing the clearing toward them, seated himself on a stump a few steps away.

"I'll listen," he said quietly, his eyes passing from Wes and falling deliberately on Jenny and Billy. Jenny tried to meet his glance but was forced to look away. His eyes were cold, and they did not seem to blink. Jenny wondered if it was natural or whether there was something wrong with his eyes.

"Was Heineken here?" Wes asked suddenly, his voice almost harsh in the warm sunlight of the clearing.

The old man glanced at him, and a dry, hacking sound burst from his lips. Jenny realized to her surprise that it was laughter.

"What if he was?"

"Is he after the money?"

The old man shook his head slowly from side to side, and his lips formed into a smile, although there was no flicker of expression in his eyes.

"What's it to you?"

"I'm wondering what Heineken knows about who killed Ed. I'm wondering if Heineken had anything to do with it. He could have arranged it."

"From jail?"

"It's been done."

"What's really on your mind, Wesley?"

"Just that. Ed was a friend."

"He was my nephew." The old man stared at Wes, and in spite of himself, Wes was forced to look away.

"So now, all of a sudden, you're concerned." He watched Wes a moment longer, then glanced at Jenny and Billy. "Who are these kids?"

"They live near me."

The old man ignored Wes, his eyes on Billy. "You have a tongue in your head, boy. Why'd you come?"

"We saw Heineken by the graveyard and heard him and his cousin talking. We told Wes, and Wes figured you ought to hear what they were saying."

"What were they saying?"

"They said they figured you knew where the money was hidden."

"And?"

"They planned to get you drunk so you'd tell them."

"And if I didn't, they had other ways they were going to get it out of me."

Billy nodded.

The old man fell silent, his eyes on the ground. Abruptly he looked at Wes. "You think I know where that money is. You think Heineken's going to get it out of me."

"Heineken won't take no for an answer."

"Maybe I don't know."

"You won't fool Heineken."

"Like I said before, what's in it for Wesley Garavoy?"

"I told you. I want to find out what went on between Heineken and Ed."

The old man looked at him, shaking his head. Abruptly he got to his feet. "I don't believe you."

He started to walk away. Wes took a step toward him, then stopped, glancing at Jenny and Billy. "All right. Heineken thinks my brother Lee turned him in. I think you know better."

"That's more like it. Come inside."

Leading the way, the old man crossed the clearing and opened the door, waiting for Jenny, Billy, and Wes to file past him. The inside of the cabin consisted of a single room with a pot-bellied stove at one end and a fireplace at the other. The floor was of packed dirt, and the furniture was basic, all of it homemade and wooden with the exception of a cast iron cot at the far end of the room, behind the stove. Against the wall opposite the door there was a long table, covered with a display of tools and implements. Billy was immediately curious and crossed the room to look more closely. Seeing his interest, the old man joined him.

"You like this stuff?" he asked gruffly.

"I do, but I don't know much about it," Billy replied hesitantly. "Did most of this come from the old village?"

"Came from all over Dover Mountain and around." The old man reached down and picked up a piece of glass. "See this piece of glass? 'Tain't like modern glass; full of ripples and bubbles. Chances are this come all the way from England. They didn't make no glass in the colonies until later."

"What's this?" Billy asked, pointing to a wooden yoke much too small for a horse or an ox.

"That's a neck yoke. They used them for carrying buckets of water from the well. Figured it would save time to carry two big buckets, and they could carry more weight by hanging it off the shoulders."

"It seems like it would be more trouble than it was worth."

"Not if you were fetchin' water all the time." The old man turned to Wes, who had seated himself on one of the upright logs that served for chairs. "So you're worried about that brother of yours."

"Lee didn't blow the whistle on Heineken. I know that."

"I expect you're right." The old man picked up the coffeepot from the stove and shook it to see if there was any left. Finding it empty, he set it down and settled on a log opposite Wes. Jenny was already sitting next to Wes, and Billy took the seat next to her. "Why don't you tell Lee to go away for a while?"

"Lee don't always listen to me. He don't want nobody to think he's spooked by Heineken."

"He's a damned fool then. Anybody who's not spooked by Heineken is crazy."

"How about you?"

The old man laughed. "I know Heineken. I know how he thinks. I'm one step ahead of him."

"I wouldn't count on that."

"What do you want me to do? Tell Heineken that Ed turned him in? He wouldn't believe me."

"Why did Ed turn him in?"

"I don't know as how he did." The old man paused, watching Wes with a slight smile. "Of course, he might have, and *if* he did, I expect it was because he didn't trust him. Ed had plans, and Heineken wasn't in them."

"I don't know why Heineken wouldn't believe that."

"Heineken's smart about a lot of things, but he never was smart about Ed. He thought he was going away with Ed. He won't believe Ed crossed him."

"Who killed Ed?"

"Ask Captain Wiley. He investigated it. Seems to me he said it was suicide."

"You and I both know it weren't no suicide."

"So?"

"So somebody killed him."

The old man turned away, and again the dry, hacking laughter sounded in the stillness. His eyes were on Jenny now, and she sensed an odd curiosity, as if he were measuring her and Billy.

"Heineken see you?" he asked suddenly.

She shook her head.

"Just as well. If I were you, Wesley, I'd take these kids down off the mountain and keep them there."

"Maybe you ought to come, too."

"Not me. I got plans for Heineken."

"You're playing with fire."

The old man studied Wes. Then abruptly he smiled and turned to Billy. "You live here long?"

"We just moved here in August."

"Dover Valley's not a bad place. When Heineken's out of the way, come up here. There's a lot to learn on this mountain." He stared at Billy, then gestured with his head behind him. "Bring me the Bible from the shelf near the fire."

Billy did as requested and set the Bible on the table in front of the old man, who reached out, running his fingers over the surface. "This Bible's been in the family a long time. It was Ed's before he was killed." He opened it but did not look down at it. "I ain't been able to read it lately. Can't see the writing no more. The writing in my own Bible was bigger, but I buried it next to the chimney, and I can't dig it out."

"Why?" Billy asked.

"Brings luck to the house to put the word of God and something of value into the foundation. If you dig it out, you queer your luck." He turned to Wes. "Wesley Garavoy, you're witness to this. If anything happens to me, this here Bible goes to this young feller. The tools, too."

Billy stared at the old man, nonplussed. "Why me?" he asked in a barely audible voice.

The old man laughed, pleased with the effect of his announcement. "Because I've taken a liking to you. At my age a man does what he wants. You hear me, Wesley?"

"I hear you."

"All right. You'd best go now. And like I say, keep these kids off the mountain. You never know where Heineken's likely to turn up."

"Are you going to tell him about Ed turning him in?" Wes asked.

"I'll tell him, but I don't know what good it will do."

"Which way was Heineken going?"

"Back to the stone house from what he said, but I wouldn't count on it." He turned to Billy. "Remember what I said. If anything happens to me, all the stuff on the table and the Bible are yours. It may not seem like much, but you never know about things. Might be more to it than meets the eye. 'Specially the Bible."

Billy thanked him, but the old man shook off his thanks and ushered them out into the sunlight. "You'd best be moving now. Which way did you come?"

"The slide and the deer trail," Wes replied.

"Might as well head back that way."

As they left the clearing, the old man was still standing in the doorway, watching them, his eyes shining in the sunlight. Billy waved at him, but he did not appear to notice.

"How well can he see?" Jenny asked Wes.

"Not too well until his eyes adjust. They tear when he first hits the sunlight. That's what makes them shine."

"He ought to see a doctor."

"Him? Not a chance."

"Why do you think he did what he did?" Billy asked.

"What?"

"Giving me all that stuff if anything happens to him?"

"I think it's like he said. He took a shine to you. Who else does he have to give it to?"

"Still seems funny."

"He's most likely feeling morbid with Heineken around. Don't know as I blame him."

"What do you think he's planning?"

"No way to know. He's a wise old codger, but I hope he knows what he's doing."

"What are you going to do about Lee?"

"I don't know yet. If I can get him to go away, I will."

"Want us to say anything to Captain Wiley?"

"Just tell him you came up here and met John Quarry. And tell him I'll keep an eye on things."

"Should we tell him what the old man said about having plans for Heineken?"

"Best not. I'd rather look into that myself."

"How?"

Wes turned to Billy. "Tell you the truth, I don't rightly know, but I guess I'll figure it out. One way or another, I'll figure it out."

8 Something Seen

When Jenny, Billy, and the two Wileys went to Apple Hill on Wednesday afternoon, they were joined by Liz Gordon and Sol Feldstein. After getting off the bus, they walked to the Drake house, and Mr. Drake set about finding jobs for the new recruits. It turned out to be an easy task, since Liz had been knitting for several years, and Sol was a good mechanic and anxious to learn about farm machinery.

As they were walking to the crafts shed, Jenny asked Diane why local kids had not worked at Apple Hill before.

"I don't know," Diane admitted. "I guess we never thought of hiring local kids until Mr. Crabtree and his people began to push us. Actually it was Dad's idea, but Mr. Carrington and the trustees were all for it. We figured the best way to counter Crabtree's lies was for people to see what Apple Hill was really like."

"How did your family happen to come to Apple Hill?"

"Dad's a social worker. He heard about it and wrote to Mr. Carrington." She laughed. "I'm glad he did. Otherwise I wouldn't be living here now. I'd be living in the Bronx."

"Have you ever hiked up Dover Mountain?" Billy asked.

"Dad and I hiked up last year. We went to the graveyard and the village, and then we looked into the mine."

"What's the mine like?"

"It's sort of like a big cave. I guess it might have been a cave originally with the mine shafts going off from it. We didn't go inside. Dad didn't have a flashlight, and there's supposed to be lots of snakes."

"How big is it?" Jenny asked. "I mean, can you stand up?"

"Sure, at least in the front part of it. We couldn't see in too far."

They had reached the shed now, and Jenny and Diane found the three girls of the sewing group sitting at the table, waiting for them. At first Jenny felt a little uneasy. Today there would be no Mrs. Smart to supervise, and she wondered whether she and Diane would be able to cope with the questions and the requests for assistance. She needn't have worried. The afternoon went well from the first.

Carrie had not been satisfied with her long-tailed dog, and she decided to do another that would not only have a long tail but floppy ears as well. She quickly became engrossed in her new project, while Phyllis started on a new Raggedy Ann doll. Polly worked with Jenny, cutting out and sewing clothes for the Barbie doll that Jenny had brought as a model. Jenny had suggested the time before that many younger girls had Barbies and similar dolls and that doll clothes might be a good sideline for local sales.

To Jenny's surprise Polly caught on quickly and soon designed an outfit of her own. While she worked, she chattered like a chipmunk, telling Jenny and the others about her home in California, where it was never cold in the winter. Jenny asked if she had written to her mother as she had intended, and Polly said she had, adding that it was probably not a very good letter, since she didn't write very well. Jenny tried to reassure her, saying that Polly's mother would welcome the letter in any case, but Polly was unconvinced.

"I hope you're right, but I don't think so," she said sadly, her cheerfulness abruptly gone. "I think my mother's ashamed of me."

"No way," Jenny said quickly, but Polly shook her head, frowning down at the table. She was silent for some time after that; and watching her, Jenny was almost sorry that she had mentioned the letter. She was trying to think of something to say when Polly looked up at her, her eyes uncommonly serious.

"Mummy hasn't written me for more than a month now," she said quietly. "The last time she wrote, she said she was sick."

"Maybe she hasn't been able to write," Jenny suggested and immediately regretted it when Polly began to wonder if her mother had been too sick to write.

"No. I just meant that when someone's been sick, they fall behind, and they have a lot of catching up to do. You'll see when your mother does write."

"I hope so." Polly stared down at the table, hands clenched tightly. "I asked her something really special this time. I asked her if I could go home for a visit. I haven't been home since she got married again. I've only seen her once." She looked up, her eyes on Jenny. "Maybe I shouldn't have asked. Maybe she doesn't want me home."

"Why wouldn't she want you home?"

"She's got a whole new family now. Maybe . . . maybe I wouldn't fit in."

Polly stared morosely at the pattern in front of her, and for an awful moment Jenny was afraid that she might burst into tears. It was Diane who came to the rescue, observing that it looked as if the dog she had just made was all tail and no dog. She held it up, and indeed the tail, curving back over the hindquarters, was so long that it practically reached to the tip of the nose. It looked delightfully perky and ridiculous, and they all had a good laugh as they looked at it. The rest of the afternoon passed with no serious difficulties, but Jenny made a note to herself to be more careful about what she said.

By the time the bell sounded to summon the kitchen crew, she and Polly had each designed and sewn a Barbie outfit, while the other girls had finished, or almost finished, their own projects. Saying goodbye to Diane and the others, Jenny hurried to the woodworking shop where she picked up Billy, and they started homeward. It was already almost dark when they reached the Garavoy house. Glancing toward the lighted windows as she passed, Jenny came to an abrupt halt.

"Look!" she whispered, catching Billy's arm.

"What?"

"Did you see it?"

"See what?"

"Someone was looking in the window."

"You're sure?"

"Yes. Come on."

Jenny hurried off, and Billy had to move quickly to keep up with her. Only when they had arrived at their own house did Jenny speak again.

"I think I know who was looking in that window," she said softly.

"Who?"

"Heineken. I recognized his profile. He had a crew cut and the same big nose."

"What do you think he was doing there?"

"Maybe he was looking for Lee."

They were on the back porch, and Billy paused, his hand on the doorknob. "I'll tell you what," he said finally. "I'll tell Wes tomorrow."

"Why not tonight?"

"Are you crazy? Wes doesn't have a telephone, and with Heineken around, I'm not going anywhere near that house. Remember what Captain Wiley said."

Jenny nodded. Billy was right. Tomorrow would be soon enough.

9 Mr. Crabtree

Over supper the next evening Jenny and Billy told their mother and father about their visit to the graveyard on Dover Mountain and the subsequent visit to John Quarry. They had intended to tell them earlier, but had put it off, since their father had been away on a business trip. Mrs. Martin was very upset.

"I'm going to have to speak to Gil Wiley," she muttered darkly. "I can't understand why he'd give his blessing to the two of you going up on that mountain with Wesley Garavoy. It could have been dangerous."

"Why was it dangerous?" Billy objected. "Heineken didn't want to be seen. He would have avoided us. Besides, Wes made sure we didn't run into him."

"It's no business for children, no matter what you say."

"It wasn't Captain Wiley's fault," Jenny said quickly. "Billy and I wanted to go. We wanted to meet John Quarry. Kids are always telling stories about Hermit John, but none of them have ever talked to him. Besides, I was the only one in my class who had never been up on Dover Mountain. Mr. Farber, the history teacher, is always telling about how they mined iron up there during the Revolution and the War of 1812."

"Did you see the mine?" Mr. Martin asked.

"No, but we spent a lot of time at the graveyard when we went up the first time. They were burying people there from 1733 to 1818."

"What did you think of John Quarry?"

"I liked him, and I think he liked us. I was scared of him at first, but then he warmed up to us. I don't think he trusts people."

"Probably doesn't."

"Do you think he was serious about giving the tools and stuff to me?" Billy asked.

"Sounds like it. What did you think, Jenny?"

"I thought he was."

"I'll talk to Wes about it, but it sounds to me as if it was your lucky day." Mr. Martin turned back to eat the last of his pie. Then he pushed back his chair and stretched. "I'll tell you the way I see it," he said softly. "I don't think you two did anything wrong in going along with Wes, but if I were you, I'd stay out of it from now on. You never know what might happen, and it strikes me that Dover Mountain is no place to be while this Heineken character and his cousin are roaming around. That meet with your approval, Betty?" He glanced at Mrs. Martin, who was silent briefly and then nodded.

"I still intend to talk to Gil Wiley," she added.

"Good enough." Mr. Martin stood up, looking at his watch. "We have a visitor due in about ten minutes time. Ever meet Mr. Crabtree?"

"The one who's trying to close down Apple Hill?"

"That's the man. If you and Billy promise to keep quiet and get to your homework right after he leaves, I'll let you sit in."

"Why's he coming?"

"He wants to talk to us about the road-straightening project." He looked at Billy. "I guess Wes Garavoy has told you about that."

Billy nodded.

Leading the way into the living room, Mr. Martin took the chair by the fire while Jenny and Billy moved to the card table and began to play gin. Mrs. Martin was just bringing the coffee in from the kitchen a few minutes later when there was a knock at the door. It was Mr. Crabtree.

Jenny's first impression, as Mr. Crabtree, his back toward her, took off his coat and hung it on the rack next to the door, was of a thin neck with wavy gray hair and slightly protruding ears. She was immediately reminded of Wes Garavoy's description: *long, scrawny neck like a chicken*. Then he turned, and to her surprise she saw an extremely good-looking man with a ready smile and considerable warmth about him. After the introductions, he settled on the sofa opposite Mr. Martin, and they chatted briefly while Mrs. Martin served the coffee. Then she sat down next to her husband, and Mr. Crabtree came to the point.

"The reason I dropped over tonight," he said, "is that at the next town meeting I intend to bring up the matter of eliminating the "S" curve this side of the Garavoy house. It's just plain dangerous, and there's no reason why we can't do something about it. I've talked to the state highway department, and they've drawn up plans, subject to local approval. I might add that they intend to upgrade Paxton Road from end to end. I don't need to tell you that that would be important for this community. It would make it much easier for farmers to haul their produce to the rail junction at Greene River."

"It would also increase the traffic," Mrs. Martin observed.

"That's true," Mr. Crabtree agreed. His voice was a deep baritone, and he spoke carefully, seeming to weigh his words. "I'm aware that that might not appeal to some residents of the town, but if you consider the overall benefits, it strikes me that it would be rather shortsighted to oppose the project on those grounds. The safety factor alone would seem decisive."

"How do you propose to eliminate the "S" curve?" Mr. Martin asked.

"The logical way is to eliminate the loop around the Garavoy property. I've already suggested to the Garavoys that we could move their house to the southeastern corner of their lot. Of course, we'd compensate them."

"How did they react?"

Mr. Crabtree laughed. "The Garavoys have never been known for reasonableness."

"What do you propose to do then?"

"If the town votes to straighten the road, the state will condemn. The Garavoys will have no choice in the matter. I'm hoping I can make them aware of that and work out something less drastic. That's why I came to you. You're friendly with the Garavoys. I thought you might speak to them."

Mr. Martin finished his coffee and set the cup back in the saucer. "Perhaps I will."

"There's one other matter." Mr. Crabtree seemed to hesitate, his eyes momentarily falling on Jenny and then passing on. "I understand your children were on Dover Mountain a few days ago and saw a man they thought was Kurt Heineken?"

Mr. Martin nodded. "That's true, although I don't know how you found out about it."

"Wes Garavoy told me." He paused. Then he turned to Jenny. "Might I ask you to describe the man for me."

Jenny glanced at her father, and catching his almost imperceptible nod, gave Mr. Crabtree the description. He remained silent for some time after she had finished. Then he stood up and walked to the fire, turned and stood with his back to it. Abruptly he laughed.

"I was hoping that the description wouldn't fit," he admitted, still smiling. "Unfortunately, it fits perfectly. Kurt Heineken is obviously back in our midst."

"Did you know him?" Jenny asked, ignoring Billy's kick under the table.

Mr. Crabtree nodded, his expression serious. "Yes, I knew him. He worked for me at one time. He's a very dangerous man. I didn't expect him to be paroled so soon. Did you tell Captain Wiley about seeing him?"

"We told him the same day."

"Good."

Mr. Crabtree stood awhile longer. Then he moved away from the fireplace, and noting that it was late, he stepped into the hall and slipped into his coat. He thanked the Martins for their hospitality and left.

"I wonder what *that* was all about?" Mrs. Martin mused, as she and Mr. Martin returned to the room.

"What do you think, Jen?" Mr. Martin asked.

"I don't know why he asked me to describe Heineken. Wes knew Heineken, and if Wes told him it was Heineken, why ask me?"

"Maybe he doesn't trust Wes," Billy suggested.

"I wonder why Wes said anything to him?"

"I'll bet I know!" Billy exclaimed. "Maybe instead of Ed Quarry, it was Mr. Crabtree who turned in Heineken. Maybe Wes was trying to trap him."

"Why would Wesley do that?" Mrs. Martin asked.

"To protect Lee. Heineken thinks Lee turned him in."

Mr. Martin nodded. "It could be, Billy, but I wouldn't say anything about it. If you're right, there may be trouble, and I don't want you to get involved in it. Understand?"

Billy nodded. "What are you going to do about the Garavoys?"

"I'll talk to Wes, and maybe we can come up with an alternate proposal."

"I'm surprised Mr. Crabtree didn't mention Apple Hill."

Mr. Martin glanced at his wife. "I'm not. I expect he knows where we stand on that matter."

"You would have thought he'd try to change our minds."

"Not him. He's a politician to his fingertips." He was silent briefly. Then he turned to Jenny and Billy. "What did we say about homework?"

"We're going now," Jenny assured him.

Getting up from the table, she left the room quickly and started up the stairs, closely followed by Billy. Before disappearing into her room, however, she motioned her brother closer.

"Did you tell Wes about seeing Heineken?" she asked in a whisper.

Billy nodded. "I think Mr. Crabtree's kind of worried," he said softly.

"If your guess is right, he's got reason to be."

"Remember what Wes told us about Mr. Crabtree hinting that he might drop the road-straightening thing if the Garavoys voted with him on Apple Hill? He didn't say anything about that tonight."

"Of course he didn't."

"Think Wes told him no?"

"Ask Wes."

"I wonder how long Heineken worked for Crabtree."

"Why?"

"I don't know. I was just thinking." Billy looked at her and abruptly grinned. "Forget it," he said and walked quickly down the hall to his own room.

Jenny watched him go, shaking her head. Sometimes Billy could be extremely irritating.

10 Rumors

When Jenny arrived at the sewing room the next day, Polly was waiting by the door with a letter tightly clutched in her hand.

"She's coming," Polly announced happily, eyes shining. "My mother will be here in four weeks. The letter came in the mail this morning."

"What does she say?"

"Here, you read it."

Jenny took the letter and read it quickly. She was surprised, although she didn't let it show. The letter was cold and almost formal. It was as if Polly's mother had not wanted to write one more word than was necessary. And it wasn't a case of simplifying to make it easier for Polly to read. The words were not simple.

"She has real nice handwriting, doesn't she?" Polly

observed, looking over Jenny's shoulder. "It's not messy like mine."

"It is nice," Jenny agreed. The letters were gently rounded, and the script was flowing and absolutely regular. "That's great news, Polly, really great!" she said, handing back the letter. "Your mother's going to be proud of you."

"I hope she will." Polly hesitated. "She doesn't say anything about me visiting her out there."

"Maybe she wants to see you first. Maybe she'd rather tell you herself."

"You think so?"

"Sure. Come on."

Throwing an arm around the blonde girl's shoulders, Jenny hurried down to where Diane and the others waited. The sewing session went well. Jenny let Polly work largely on her own, while she worked with Phyllis who was doing her first animal. Diane had her hands full at first. Carrie had suddenly become very discouraged, and Diane had to tease and coax her out of her depression. It took some doing, but Carrie finally regained her normal composure and became engrossed in making a long-tailed ginger cat with a fat tummy. As usual they were disappointed when the bell rang, signaling the end of the session. After the campers had gone, Jenny and Diane walked over to the woodworking shop to wait for Billy. On the way Jenny asked about Carrie.

"Does she get like that often?"

"Only once in a while. Most of them do."

"Why?"

"Lots of reasons." Diane returned the greeting of a camper, then turned back to Jenny. "Think of it this way. The campers may be retarded, but they feel things just like we do. It's not easy for them, being away from their families, and if the people who are important to them don't come through, it can get them down. Like I might be in a bad mood, but if Sammy there waves at me, and I ignore him, that's not good. Polly's way up now because her mother wrote to say she's coming, but what happens if she doesn't come?"

"She wouldn't do that."

"She's already done it once. We had a rough couple of days with Polly."

"Why didn't her mother come?"

"I don't know. Some parents really stick with their kids, but others don't. I guess because their kid's retarded, they think it's some kind of a black mark against them. It's too bad. These kids need to know that someone cares."

"Do you think Polly's mother will come this time?"

"I hope so, but I'll tell you what Dad told me. He said to try to keep Polly from getting too high."

Jenny nodded, remembering Polly's excitement about the letter. It wasn't going to be easy.

"Hey, here's Billy."

Jenny looked up to see Billy and Drew emerging from the woodworking shed.

"Is your father home?" Jenny asked Drew as he came up to them.

"Yeah. Why?"

"I was just wondering."

"Want to talk to him?"

Jenny nodded.

"What about?"

Jenny laughed. "Nothing special. We just want to ask him about something. Are you and Debbie ready?"

Debbie came toward them a few minutes later. "Liz is all involved in a project," Debbie told them. "She said to go on."

So the four set off together.

"Did you two really see Heineken on Dover Mountain?" Drew asked.

"Who told you?" Jenny asked, startled.

"I heard it at school," Drew said, evasively. "Debbie did, too."

Debbie nodded and looked at Jenny and Billy expectantly. But neither said anything. Instead Jenny mentioned something about one of the girls at school, and the conversation moved off in another direction.

When they reached the Wiley house, Jenny and Billy were relieved to see Captain Wiley's car parked in the driveway. Debbie and Drew took them in and called to Captain Wiley. He came to the door of his office.

"I've been expecting you for the last couple of days," he said with a smile. "Come on in." They walked in, and he closed the door behind them, leaving Debbie and Drew outside.

"I take it you've met John Quarrry."

Jenny nodded.

"Want to tell me about it?"

For the next five minutes Jenny described their afternoon on Dover Mountain, leaving nothing out. Captain Wiley listened carefully, jotting down an occasional note. When she had finished, he sat silently, considering what she had told him. Finally Captain Wiley stood up and crossed the room to where a local map was mounted on the wall. He studied it carefully. Then he walked to the window and sat on the ledge.

"Did John Quarry say anything more about this plan of his?"

"No. All he said was that he had a plan."

"Did he seem confident?"

"Very."

Captain Wiley frowned down at the floor. "I wish I knew what the old geezer is up to," he muttered.

"Why don't you ask him?" Billy questioned.

Captain Wiley laughed. "Wouldn't do me any good. Old John's as independent as they come. If he's decided to play a lone hand, that's the way he'll play it. Knowing him, I figured he would from the first. I was just hoping I might be able to get some clue as to what he had in mind."

"Maybe Wes knows."

"I doubt it. I doubt if Wes knows anything more than you do."

He looked toward the road, then stood up and walked back to the desk. After surveying his notes, he turned to Billy. "John must have taken quite a shine to you, Billy. If I remember correctly, he's got a fair collection of colonial and Indian tools. He's been picking them up for years. There must be some value to that collection."

"Has he always lived up on the mountain?" Billy asked.

"Ever since I've been here."

"Why?"

"Who knows? People have their own reasons for doing things. He's an independent sort, and I guess he likes being where no one interferes with him. I suspect that when he wants venison, he shoots a deer, and he doesn't worry overmuch whether it's in season. I suppose I should do something about it, but I never have. Bill Kovac, the game warden for this part of the country, feels the same way. Old John is the last of a breed, and since he doesn't do any harm or waste anything, we're just as glad to let him be."

"He must live pretty much the way the miners used to live up there."

"Yes and no. It was a lot different for them."

"Why?"

"It was pretty grim up there in colonial times. Working in a mine is a rough way of life. The men who worked the mine were baked in the summer and frozen in the winter. You don't know what cold is until you've been up there on a winter day. They weren't free either. They were debtors. The Tooks family brought them from England as indentured servants. They worked long shifts, and if they got sick, that was their hard luck. It was hard for the women and children, too. They had to raise what food they could and haul the water and weave and sew and darn. It was a hard life. In fact, it got so bad at one point that the miners revolted."

"What happened?"

"The Tooks family called in the Redcoats. They went up the mountain, caught the ringleaders, and hung them on the village green down here in Dover Valley. That was the end of it."

Jenny and Billy stared at him, while he nodded grimly. "There was a lot of bad blood around here in colonial times. You don't always get it from the history books, but people like the Tookses ran things to suit themselves."

"How come they stopped working the mine?" Billy asked.

"The surface ore ran out. Besides, it cost too much to mine and smelt the iron here." He paused to light a cigar and puffed energetically to get it going. Then he turned back to Billy. "Anyway, as I was saying, the old man seems to have singled you out. If I were you, I'd keep my eyes and ears open. He may try to contact you."

"Why?"

"I don't know, but he may. For instance, if he knows where the money's hidden and he's frightened enough of Heineken, he may decide to tell you."

Billy stared at him, his eyes wide. "Why me?"

"Your guess is as good as mine." He stared at Billy for a moment before turning to Jenny. "Anything else on your mind?"

"I saw Kurt Heineken looking in the Garavoys' window two nights ago. At least, I think it was Kurt Heineken."

"Probably was. Wes and I have persuaded Lee to go away for a while."

"Where?"

"Downstate. Neil Bishop needed someone to pick up some equipment for him. It seemed like a good job for Lee. Well, I guess that does it for now. Let me know if anything else comes your way. And one thing—" He looked up, catching Jenny's eye—"keep off the mountain. There's no telling what's going to happen, and I don't want you two running into Heineken."

"A lot of people seem to know that we ran into him."

Captain Wiley smiled, leaning back and stretching. "That's my doing," he admitted. "I want people to know that Heineken's around and where he is."

"I thought you didn't want people to know."

"A man can change his mind, can't he?"

Jenny's last impression as she left the room was of Captain Wiley's face almost obscured by a cloud of smoke. He looked positively devilish.

11 Jenny Writes a Letter

During the next few weeks Jenny and Billy had little time to think about Heineken and Dover Mountain. The homework burden had been gradually increasing, and Billy was playing football, while Jenny had a role in her class play.

The job at Apple Hill, too, was becoming more demanding. Jenny's and Diane's sewing group was now up to six, and Billy and Drew had three campers apiece for whom they served as Assistant Counselor. Billy saw Wes Garavoy occasionally and asked about Heineken and John Quarry, but Wes only shook his head and told him there was nothing new.

It was three weeks to the day after Polly had received the letter from her mother that Diane pulled Jenny aside at recess.

"Guess what?" she reported, smiling grimly. "Polly's mother isn't coming."

Jenny stared at her. "You're sure?"

"She sent a telegram this morning saying that she wouldn't be able to make it."

"How's Polly taking it?"

"Not too well. She was really counting on it."

"I wonder what happened."

"No telling. I figured I'd better tell you."

"Will she be coming to sewing?"

"Sure."

Jenny looked up as the bell signaled the end of recess.

"Do you have an address for Polly's mother?" she asked.

"I think so. Why?"

"I'm going to write her."

Diane stared at Jenny in surprise. Then abruptly she broke into a wide grin. "Right on, Jenny Martin, right on! I'll give you the address when we get to Apple Hill."

Giving Jenny a playful punch on the arm, she hurried off to class, while Jenny walked slowly to the library. She had a free period, and homework done, she was already formulating what she was going to write. It was simple really. If she could make Polly's mother see how much Polly cared about her home and family, Mrs. Carillo's own conscience would do the rest. After all, she was Polly's mother, and Polly needed a mother. Jenny didn't question the rightness of her writing, although later when she told Billy about it, he did.

"It's none of your business," he argued. "I don't think Mr. Carrington will like it."

"It's not coming from Mr. Carrington. It's coming from me. If I want to write Polly's mother, I have a perfect right to."

Billy turned away with a shrug. "It's on your head."

When Jenny went to Apple Hill that afternoon, she took the letter with her, and before going to the sewing room, she got the address from Diane, put it on the envelope, stamped it, and dropped it in the mailbox.

"You know, it just might work," Diane remarked thoughtfully.

"Once she sees Polly, she'll come around."

"Yeah. The trick is to get her here. Your letter might do it."

"Think it was too strong?"

Diane shook her head. "No way. Come on. We'd better get over to the sewing room."

When they reached the sewing room, it was a subdued group of campers who awaited them. Jenny and Diane sat down as if nothing unusual had occurred. During the two hour session, Polly spoke little and worked more slowly than usual. Several times she seemed on the verge of tears, but Diane had turned her radio to a disco station, and she and Jenny worked hard at keeping the mood upbeat. Only at the end when the bell sounded, calling the kitchen crew, did Jenny pull Polly aside to say that she had heard the news.

"I know you're disappointed, but wait until your mother writes. It just may be that she's had to postpone the trip. You know, it's a long way from California."

"She was going to come one other time."

"I know, but this will be different."

Polly shook her head sadly. "It's what I said before. She doesn't want me. I wouldn't fit."

"You'd fit. Once she comes, she'll see it."

Polly shook her head, but said nothing. After a moment, Diane, who had been watching, reminded her that she was on kitchen crew. Polly thanked Diane, and giving Jenny a parting smile, hurried off. When she had disappeared, Diane told Jenny that Billy was looking for her.

"Why?"

"I don't know. He said he'd wait for you down at the entrance. He walked down there with Sol."

"I'd better get going then. See you tomorrow at school."

When Jenny reached the gate, she found Billy sitting on a rock next to the road.

"What's up?" she asked as she came up to him.

"Wes came by the woodworking shop this afternoon. He says he wants to see us."

"Wes Garavoy came here? It must be pretty important."

"That's what I figure."

"What did he say?"

"Nothing. He just said for us to come by after we finished school tomorrow."

"That's all?"

"That's all."

"What did you tell him?"

"I said we would."

Jenny laughed. "Guess we will then."

12 The Oldest Knows Best

When Jenny and Billy arrived at the Garavoy house the next afternoon, they found Wes working on his car. He slid out from under it and stood up as they walked toward him, reaching down to pet Skipper.

"What does your dog do while you're at school?" he asked.

"He waits for us back at the house."

"Been home then?"

"Yes. We left our schoolbooks before walking over."

Wes gave Skipper a final pat before straightening and stretching. "Want to come up on the mountain with me?" he asked casually.

Jenny glanced at Billy. She was about to say *yes*, but then she remembered what her parents and Captain Wiley had said. They had both been firm in their insistence that she and Billy keep away from Dover Mountain. Looking at Billy, she could tell that he was thinking along the same lines. She turned to Wes.

"We'd like to, Wes, but we've been told to stay off the mountain, and not just by our parents but by Captain Wiley, too."

"What if I told you that Lee's gone to get Captain Wiley, and that they'll be meeting us up there?"

"When did Lee get back?" Billy asked.

"This morning. I called him."

Billy looked at Jenny. "What about Heineken?"

"We won't run into Heineken. I can promise you that."

"Should we take Skipper home?"

Wes looked at Skipper, a twinkle in his eye. "Don't intend to shoot nothing this afternoon. Might as well take him with us. Looks like he could use a run."

"Will we be seeing John Quarry?"

"We'll be going to his house."

"What's it all about?" Jenny asked, irritated by Wes' evasiveness.

Wes laughed drily. "You'll see soon enough." He punched the lid down on a can of grease, wiped his hands on the old shirt he was using as a rag, and put away his tools. Then, asking if they were ready, he set off, and they fell into step behind him.

As usual Wes set a fast pace, and it was all they could do to keep up with him. They were already puffing when he called a halt at the gap in the stone wall above Mrs. Ingersol's orchard.

"Where are we meeting Captain Wiley?" Billy asked.

"He's meeting us at John Quarry's house." Wes looked up at the sky, then picked up a dead leaf and released it, watching its fluttering descent to the ground. "It's going to snow. Heavy, too."

"How do you know?"

"Air's thick, and it's dead still. Can't hear no birds nor nothing."

"When do you think it will start?"

"Anytime now. We'd best get a move on."

The climb to the cliff took twenty minutes. Here they stopped to catch their breath before scrambling up the final grade to the plateau. To Jenny's and Billy's surprise, Wes did not take the path that skirted the cliff edge, but followed the old road instead. They passed the stone house and the graveyard, but Wes did not stop. Finally, when they had almost reached the deserted village, he turned off on a narrow path that led to the northeast.

"Where are we going?" Billy managed to gasp out between labored breaths.

"I told you. John Quarry's house," Wes called back. "It's not far now."

Five minutes later they stepped into the clearing in front of the cabin. It looked much as it had on their first visit, except that this time there was no smoke issuing from the burn barrel. A slight breeze had come up, and the air was sprinkled with tiny snowflakes. Over to their right Jenny could see the entrance to the trail that they had taken the first time. Skipper had been investigating it, and now he moved toward the house, trotting in his usual purposeful way.

"I guess you two are pretty curious by now," Wes said suddenly, glancing back at them. "I'll tell you what's up as soon as we've had a look in the cabin."

"Where's John Quarry?"

"Like I said, I'll tell you in a minute."

Crossing the clearing, Wes opened the door, followed by Skipper, Billy and Jenny. Wes walked around the room quickly, as if looking for something, while the others watched him. Finally Billy asked him what he was looking for.

"I thought Old John might have left a note for us. He told me to get on up here if anything happened to him."

"Has something happened to him?"

Wes sat down on one of the upturned logs that served as chairs. "He's dead," he said quietly.

Billy stared at him. "How do you know?"

"He laid a trap for Heineken, and he sprung it yesterday."

"What kind of trap?"

Wes turned to Jenny, smiling slightly. "The one kind of trap that figured to catch Heineken. He baited it with the money and made himself the hostage."

"What do you mean?"

"Heineken was on the lookout for any tricks. The one thing he didn't figure was that Old John hated him so much he didn't mind being killed himself so long as Heineken was killed with him. That's how he got him. All Heineken could think of was the money."

"You think it's true that Heineken killed John Quarry's son?"

Wes looked at Billy. "I expect it is. There was a girl mixed up in it, and Heineken was hot-tempered in those days. He had a dog would as soon bite you as look at you, and he was that way himself. That's why people were afraid of him. Young Quarry took his girl, and Heineken swore he'd get him."

"What did Ed Quarry do about it?" Billy asked.

"Nothing. That's why people figured Ed and John Quarry were on the outs, but I guess Ed squared it with Old John. Anyway, John's been leading Heineken on, making Heineken think he was forcing the truth out of him. Near as I can tell, he must've told him that the money was buried down the old mine shaft. Yesterday morning Heineken and his cousin marched him over there to show them, only what Heineken didn't know was that Old John had wired the shafts with dynamite. Once he had Heineken in the mine, he set it off."

"How do you know?"

"I was up here, watching. I saw them go to the mine, and then I heard the explosion. No one could've got out of there alive. The entrance is blocked off. Captain

Wiley's got a crew digging it out now. Billy, fetch that Bible and let me look at it."

Billy walked over to the shelf above the stove and took down the Bible. He carried it across to Wes and handed it to him. Wes opened it and began to go through it, fanning the pages from back to front.

"What are you doing?"

"Seeing if there's any message stuck into here. Uh-huh, I thought so."

Billy and Jenny watched as Wes extracted a yellowed piece of paper from the Bible and held it gingerly in front of him. "Looks like a poem." He turned to Jenny. "See if you can make any sense of it."

Jenny took the paper almost fearfully and studied the six lines, written in a round, easy-to-read script, her lips forming the words as she read.

"Read it aloud, Jenny," Billy urged.

Jenny glanced at her brother. Then she studied the paper again, puzzling out one or two words before reading it to them.

"High on the mountain,
Over the valley,
Beyond all pain, in eternal rest,
The elders wait
For the Second Coming;
What it will bring, the oldest knows best."

For a moment after Jenny had finished, no one spoke. Then Skipper barked, and seconds later they heard the sound of approaching voices. Wes jumped up and walked to the door to look out. He watched intently, then turned to Jenny.

"Put that poem in your pocket and don't say nothing about it."

"Why?"

"I don't rightly know, but I have a feeling Old John wanted for us to find that. I want to think about it a bit before we go saying anything."

Jenny nodded and put the slip of paper carefully in her pocket. When Captain Wiley came up to the door with two men a few seconds later, the three of them were sitting around the table waiting for him.

13 A Question of Conscience

So what did you find?" Wes asked as Captain Wiley stepped into the room. The two men who had been with him remained outside.

"We haven't found anything yet. He really had that place wired. It's a lot to dig through."

"Think anyone could've survived?"

"I doubt it. They would have suffocated if they weren't killed outright." He glanced around the room, his eyes returning to Wes. "How come you brought the kids here?"

"I wanted to have a look at the cabin, and since Billy's going to inherit most of the stuff, I thought I'd take him with me."

"Did you find anything?"

Wes hesitated for a fraction of a second, then shook

his head. "Nope. Whatever secrets Old John had, he took with him."

Captain Wiley nodded, and picking up the Bible from the table in front of him, began to thumb through it. Jenny and Billy exchanged a quick glance. They didn't know what Wes was up to, and they were both uneasy at being party to a lie. Jenny could feel the poem burning a hole in her pocket, and she was already playing with the possibilities. The reference to the graveyard appeared obvious. If the poem were intended as a clue, the graveyard was probably where the Quarry loot was hidden, and if she could figure it out, Wes could, too. Why did he want to keep it from Captain Wiley? Did he hope to get it for himself? It didn't make sense. He would have been wiser to come to the cabin alone if that were the case. She glanced at Wes, but he was watching Billy, who was studying the collection of tools on the bench against the wall.

"Where's Lee?" Wes asked, turning to Captain Wiley.

"He's at the mine, working with Phil Soames and Gus Walters. We'd better be getting back there." He stood up, his eyes sweeping the room. Then he stepped over to where Billy was standing in front of the bench. "Quite a collection, isn't it? You're lucky, Billy. There's not much of this kind of stuff around."

"I still can't figure why he said I should have it," Billy murmured in a puzzled tone. "I only met him once."

"The timing was right. It's simple as that. He had no one else; and when he saw you were interested, I guess he decided it might as well be you."

"I'm glad he did."

"I want to go over everything in this cabin tomorrow. Then we'll pack up the stuff and bring it down to you. Okay?"

"Sure. Thanks."

"Let's get back to the mine now."

Turning to the door, he stepped outside, and calling the two men who had come with him, started down the path toward the road. Wes and the two Martins followed more slowly. Wes seemed to be delaying on purpose, and Jenny finally asked him why he was walking so slowly.

"Figured I'd let Wiley get a little ways ahead so we could talk."

"Why didn't you want us to tell him about the poem?" Billy asked.

"Let me look at it again?" Wes requested, ignoring Billy's question.

Jenny handed it to him, and Wes read it over, frowning in concentration. "Seems like he's talking about the graveyard," he said finally.

"Do you think John Quarry wrote it?"

Wes shook his head. "Nope, not his handwriting. Looks to me like it was written by Ed Quarry."

"Then . . ."

Wes looked at Billy and laughed. "Yep. Most likely

the money's buried somewhere in that old graveyard. I figured there might be some message in the Bible from the way John Quarry talked the day we come up here."

"It's one of three things," Jenny said, looking down at the poem that Wes had handed back to her. "Either it's buried at the grave of the one who was born first, or the one who lived longest, or the one who died first."

Wes nodded. "I expect that's the case."

"So why don't you want to tell Captain Wiley?" Billy asked, returning to his original question.

"I intend to tell him"—Wes glanced at Billy over his shoulder and winked—"only I want to have a look first."

"Why?"

Wes did not answer immediately, and Billy was on the verge of repeating the question when Wes stopped, motioning them closer. He looked around carefully to make sure they were alone.

"Not everyone knows it," he said softly, keeping his voice low, "but Lee was mixed up with the gang for a while. I talked him out of it, and Ed backed me up. We'd been kids together, Ed and I, and he played it my way. Heineken and the others didn't like it, but Ed was the boss, and what he said went. The thing is, when that money is found, I want to be sure there's nothing to tie Lee into it."

"Why would there be?"

"Ed was a funny guy. He laid off Lee during his

lifetime because I asked him to, but that don't guarantee that he didn't leave a kicker behind him. He didn't like Lee leaving the gang any better than Heineken and the rest."

"How come you're telling us?"

Wes laughed. "That's a good question, ain't it? Reason is I like you, and I trust you, and I want someone with me when I check out that graveyard. Lee's played it straight from the time he left the Quarry gang. I figure what no one knows ain't going to hurt them. Captain Wiley may think Lee was tied in with the Quarrys, but I don't want him to have anything in writing that says so. Lee was a kid then, and he didn't know any better."

Jenny glanced at Billy. It made sense, but she was still a little puzzled. It seemed as if Captain Wiley should be told.

"Come on," Wes said, abruptly turning away. "Let's go to the mine."

Wes set off quickly, walking at his usual rapid pace, and Jenny and Billy had to hustle to keep up. Reaching the road, they turned right and were soon walking through the deserted village. Jenny carefully studied what was left of the foundations as they passed by.

"Why did they have foundations?" she asked. It would have been easier to build right on the ground."

"They did build on the ground at first," Wes replied. "They dug foundations later to store stuff. It kept the houses drier, too; drier and warmer."

"Doesn't seem like there were many houses."

"There were a lot more, but the others didn't have foundations."

Jenny walked on, her mind returning to the question of whether or not she should tell Captain Wiley about the poem. She had no great liking for Lee, but she liked Wes very much, and she was reluctant to act contrary to his wishes. On the other hand, the poem, if they were correct, was a vital piece of evidence, and they had no business withholding it. Indeed, the more she thought about it, the less she felt she had a choice. After all, the Quarry loot . . . Jenny looked around her uneasily, trying to shake off the sudden unsettling thought that had come to her. *That money would represent a great temptation, and only she and Billy would know that Wes had found it.* But that was ridiculous. Wes could have searched the cabin without bringing Billy and herself as witnesses. Jenny glanced at Wes walking ahead of her with long, easy strides. No, it would be better all around to tell Captain Wiley. She could figure out how later.

Captain Wiley was standing at what had been the entrance to the mine as they stepped into a clearing. Jenny looked around the clearing, and her eyes were rivetd by two blanket-covered forms lying side by side on the ground. She looked away quickly. Skipper tried to investigate at closer range, but Captain Wiley shooed him away.

"Which ones you found?" Wes asked.

"Heineken and his cousin."

"Any sign of Old John?"

"They think they've found him. They're trying to get him out now."

"How did he set it off?"

"Not sure. See that box there?"

He pointed to a box three feet long, a foot wide, and a foot deep, which was lying slightly to the right of the two blanket-covered shapes.

"They found that under Heineken."

"Anything in it?"

Captain Wiley smiled. "Odds and ends. Nothing of value. Old John may have lit the fuse while they were distracted with the box."

Wes nodded. "Could be. He couldn't see too well in the daylight, but he had eyes like a cat in the dark."

"Think they got him now."

As Captain Wiley spoke, Lee and another man emerged from the tunnel carrying a blanket-wrapped figure. They set it down beside the other two, then stood to one side. Captain Wiley stooped down, lifted the corner of the blanket, and looked.

"I guess that does it," he said softly, getting to his feet. "Wes, could I ask you and Lee to help my boys take these bodies down to the road? I'll take the kids back with me."

Wes glanced at Jenny and Billy. He seemed to hesitate, but he realized that there was no alternative, and he agreed. After speaking briefly to his men, Captain Wiley told Jenny and Billy to follow him and started down the old road. They walked rapidly. Captain Wiley seemed preoccupied and did not speak, and half-trotting along behind him, Jenny was asking herself how to broach the subject of the poem. Of course, she could have told him in so many words, but she was reluctant to do that. It would be a flat betrayal of Wes Garavoy's confidence, and yet, she wanted Captain Wiley to know. They stopped once at the top of the cut, but there was no opportunity to talk. Skipper arrived in the instant after they had stopped, and by the time she had finished petting him, Captain Wiley was on his feet urging them on. They did not stop again until they reached the road and Captain Wiley's car.

"Get in," he said curtly, opening the back door for them.

Jenny and Billy climbed in with Skipper on the seat between them, and Captain Wiley slid in behind the wheel. It was beginning to snow heavily now. Making a "U" turn, he drove down Paxton Road, pulling to a stop when he reached the Martins' driveway. Flipping the ignition off, he turned to face them.

"Well, what have you got to tell me?" he asked, a twinkle in his eye.

Relieved, Jenny smiled back at him. "How did you know?"

"I noticed the way Wes hesitated when I asked if you had found anything. I also noticed the place in the Bible where a piece of paper must have been stuck for a good many years. Other than that I was guessing."

"Here's what we found," Jenny said, handing him the slip of paper with the poem written on it.

Captain Wiley took it, and holding it to the light, read it carefully.

"Wes said it's Ed Quarry's handwriting," Jenny noted.

"So it's the old graveyard." Captain Wiley studied the piece of paper thoughtfully, then folded it and put it in his pocket. "How come Wes didn't want you to give this to me?"

Jenny glanced at Billy uneasily, and catching the look, Captain Wiley nodded grimly. "Trying to protect Lee again. I'll tell you what. I'll have a talk with Wes and straighten this out. Then we'll check the graveyard."

"Will you tell Wes how you knew about it?" Billy asked.

"I'll tell Wes. I want to talk to him anyway. There's still something that needs to be cleared up."

"What?"

"Who killed Ed Quarry. I had hoped Kurt Heineken would find me the answer, but it didn't work out that way. Maybe Wes and I can put something together."

He was silent briefly, staring straight ahead of him through the windshield. Then he glanced back at them again. "Okay, hop out now. I've got things to do."

As Jenny and Billy stepped up on the porch, Captain Wiley again made a "U" turn and drove back the way he had come.

14 A Change of Mind

For the next week Jenny and Billy anxiously awaited news, but there was no word. The snowfall had been less heavy than expected, but the ten inches that fell were more than sufficient to delay any attempt to investigate the old graveyard. Billy saw Wes Garavoy on Monday and was relieved to discover that Wes harbored no grudge. When Billy started to explain about the poem, Wes cut him short, saying that he and Captain Wiley had worked things out.

"Gil Wiley's all right," Wes said firmly. "I'm working with him on this thing; Lee and me both."

Of course Billy asked more questions, but Wes neatly avoided them, and Billy was forced to continue on his way, curiosity unsatisfied.

On Wednesday Diane rushed up to Jenny at recess.

"Guess what!" she exclaimed excitedly. "Your letter worked! Polly's mother is coming on Monday!"

"When did you hear?"

"She telephoned yesterday. She's flying to New York City and driving up in a rented car."

"Did you tell Polly?"

"Yes." Diane looked at Jenny and grinned. "She wants to meet you. She said she particularly wants to meet Jenny Martin."

"Did you tell your father about my letter?"

"Him and Mr. Carrington both. They're real pleased."

"Are you sure Polly's mother isn't angry about my writing her?"

"Why should she be angry?"

"She might think that it was none of my business."

Diane looked at Jenny and became serious. "You made it your business because of Polly, and if Mrs. Carillo can't recognize that, that's her problem. Polly's a terrific kid, and you're doing Mrs. Carillo a favor. She's darned lucky to have Polly, and it's time she knew it."

"Have you ever met her?" Jenny asked curiously.

"Nope. All I know is that Polly's father was killed in Korea, and Mrs. Carillo remarried. Her husband already had two kids, and they've had another since they were married. Dad says she's real nice in her way, but she has a hard time making decisions. I guess that's why she's only visited once since she remarried."

"Does she pay for Polly?"

"I don't know." Hearing the bell, Diane glanced at the clock on the wall above her. "I've got to go. We're having a test in French."

"You prepared?"

Diane laughed. "I hope so. See you on the bus."

Jenny watched Diane hurry away. Then she picked up her books and walked toward her American History class. She felt a warm glow of satisfaction, but she was worried, too. It could still go wrong, and whatever happened, she didn't want to see Polly hurt.

15 A Persistent Poet

When Jenny and Billy climbed off the school bus that afternoon, the first thing they noticed was a police car parked in the driveway.

"Looks like Captain Wiley's car," Billy commented as they climbed the steps toward the house.

"Maybe they've found something."

Leaving their books on the counter in the back room, they hurried to the front of the house. Captain Wiley was sitting on the chair next to the fireplace with Mr. and Mrs. Martin seated across from him.

"Here they are," Mrs. Martin said as Jenny and Billy entered the room. "Captain Wiley wanted to see you," she added in explanation.

"Have you found anything?" Jenny asked quickly, taking the chair next to him.

"Yes and no. We have found something, but it doesn't seem to solve our problems."

"What did you find?"

"Another poem." He smiled ruefully, sitting back in his chair. "Actually I'd be inclined to think the whole thing was an outsize practical joke—sort of a public last laugh from John Quarry—if Wes and Lee weren't positive that both the poems are in Ed Quarry's handwriting."

"Where did you find the second one?" Jenny asked.

"Where you said we would. The poem was locked in a strongbox and buried in the first grave to have been dug. Actually the box was inserted in the rib cage exactly where the heart would have been."

"Had it been buried a long time?"

"Far as we could tell." He reached in his pocket and pulled out a slip of paper, which he held under the lamp to read. "My fortune and my will are buried at Apple Hill." He looked up. "It's signed Ed Quarry."

"That's all?"

Captain Wiley glanced at Mr. Martin, who had asked the question, and laughed. "That's all. It doesn't tell us where or how. Just that it's buried at Apple Hill, and I don't have to tell you that Apple Hill is a fair-sized farm."

"What do you intend to do?"

"To tell you the truth, I'm not quite sure. Obviously we can't go over to Apple Hill and just start digging up the place. That's why I'm here." He turned to

Jenny and Billy. "I want you to think back to the afternoon you visited John Quarry. Can you think of anything that he said or did that might give us a hint."

"Are you sure that he even knew?"

"No, I'm not sure. That's part of the problem. I'm guessing. Nonetheless, I find it hard to believe that Ed Quarry wouldn't have left something a little more specific."

"Why do you think he went in for this hocus-pocus in the first place?" Mr. Martin asked.

"To give himself time in case someone was trying to force it out of him. Don't forget that Heineken was still on the loose when he buried the money, and besides he must have had a fence to dispose of the stolen goods. He may have been afraid that the guy who fenced for him might pull in some strong-arm help to try to get the whole pot."

"Did you look through the stuff in John Quarry's shack?" Billy asked.

"We're still going through it." Captain Wiley smiled suddenly. "He has some nice pieces, Billy. You'll be getting a nice collection."

"I still can't believe that he gave it to me."

"Look at it this way. He knew what he was planning for Heineken, and that he wouldn't survive it. He wanted someone to have that stuff; someone who would be interested and would keep it up, and who might even add to it. He decided you looked like the best bet, and since he didn't have much time, he made up his mind then and there. The question is did he say anything else? For instance, could there be some other clue besides the poem in the Bible? It's possible that that was intended as a false lead."

"Are you sure something else isn't buried in the graveyard?"

"We've been checking that out for the last three days. We don't intend to stop until we're absolutely positive there's nothing buried there besides the people." He was silent briefly. Then he stood up and stretched. "What I want you two to do is to think about your talk with Old John. If you come up with something, let me know. Okay?"

Jenny and Billy nodded solemnly.

Satisfied, Captain Wiley turned to Mr. and Mrs. Martin. "Are you coming to the town meeting next Wednesday?"

Mrs. Martin smiled. "We wouldn't miss it."

"Can we go?" Jenny asked quickly.

"I don't know. I've never been to a town meeting." Mrs. Martin turned to Captain Wiley. "Can we take Jenny and Billy?"

"Sure. I always take Debbie and Drew. It's an important thing for them to see."

"Are they going to bring up the road straightening?" Billy asked.

"I don't know. Only the Board of Selectmen knows the agenda, and they haven't said anything to me. Fact is, I make it a point not to ask. Once people are there though, anyone can bring up anything that's on his or her mind."

Captain Wiley reached down to pick up his brief-case. "Remember, if you two think of anything that might help, let me know. I don't want to go near Apple Hill until I have a better idea of what I'm about. And Billy, we'll bring the stuff from John Quarry tomorrow. You ought to think about where you're going to put it."

"I will," Billy promised.

Giving them a final smile, Captain Wiley started toward the door, accompanied by Mr. and Mrs. Martin. As they left the room, Jenny turned to Billy, asking if he had any ideas.

Billy shook his head. "I'll go through John Quarry's Bible when they bring it down. Maybe he's got some passage marked."

"They've probably done that already."

"They may have missed something."

Jenny reached down to pet Skipper. "It's probably something real simple," she said thoughtfully. "That's what makes it so hard."

"Maybe it isn't. Maybe it's like Captain Wiley said. Maybe it's a joke on everybody. Maybe there isn't any money."

Jenny stared at Billy, turning the thing over in her mind. It was crazy, but it just could be possible.

"If it's a joke," she said softly, "I don't think any-one's going to be laughing."

Billy grinned broadly. "That's for sure."

16 Doll for a Sister

For the next two schooldays and over the weekend Jenny and Billy waited eagerly for something to happen, but nothing did. Captain Wiley finally abandoned the graveyard and John Quarry's house, convinced that nothing was hidden in either place, and pronounced himself at a dead end until and unless he or Jenny or Billy could think of a new direction to take. Billy, for his part, went over the Bible page by page, but he could find no markings or notations of any kind. A close examination of the tools and weapons in John Quarry's collection proved equally fruitless.

It was on Monday as they were walking up the Apple Hill driveway that a thought struck Billy, and he stopped dead in his tracks. Jenny and others turned to ask what was wrong, but he shrugged it off, saying that he had stubbed his toe. Before they went to the craft rooms, however, Billy pulled Jenny aside.

"I just had an idea," he said, keeping his voice low. "It doesn't make sense that Ed Quarry would have bothered to write two poems. What if someone found the first poem and dug up the money that was buried in the graveyard? Then, instead of throwing the box in which the money was buried away, he put it back down the hole with the note about Apple Hill in it and covered it up again."

"Why would he do that?"

"So no one would know that he had found the money."

"Why wouldn't he just tear up the first poem after he found the money?"

"Because then people would be looking all over for the money. This way anyone who found the second poem would think the money was still buried, only at Apple Hill instead of in the graveyard."

"But didn't Wes and Lee say that the second poem was in Ed Quarry's handwriting, too?"

"The poem's short. Whoever found the money could have forged it."

Jenny thought it over, and she had to admit Billy had a point. "It could be, but it also could be that the money *is* buried here at Apple Hill."

"But where?"

Jenny smiled. "Who knows? Come on. We'd better get to work."

The sewing group was already gathered around Diane when Jenny arrived. Polly saw Jenny and moved quickly to her side, her face flushed with excitement. "My mother's coming this afternoon. She called from New York, and she's on the way."

Jenny had forgotten in the rush of events that this was the day of Mrs. Carillo's visit, and she glanced quickly at Diane who grinned back at her. "Polly's designed a real cute skirt and blouse outfit for a Barbie doll. She's hoping to get it done before her mother arrives."

"How long is she staying?' Jenny asked.

"Until tomorrow," Polly replied.

"Did you talk to her?"

"No. Mr. Carrington did."

"Well, if you're going to finish, we'd better get to work."

The session went well. Polly's high spirits were infectious, and the girls chatted merrily as they worked. Carrie was making an elephant, and she and Diane argued cheerfully over the proportions, Diane maintaining that a long trunk might have lots of advantages, but that no self-respecting elephant would have a trunk so long that he'd trip over it when he walked. Observing Phyl's labors, Bitsy, a new girl to the group, said that the neck on Phyl's giraffe looked more like an elephant's trunk. Phyl's feelings were hurt, but she was mollified when Diane pointed out that a giraffe's neck is actually an elephant trunk with a head on it, and once Phyl had sewed and stuffed the head, the neck would look like a proper neck.

Although Polly took an active part in the flow of conversation, she worked rapidly, sewing the outfit she had designed with close attention to detail.

"I have a little half-sister I've never seen," she explained, "and I want to give my mother this outfit to take back to her."

"Why don't you give her this doll, too?" Jenny suggested, pointing to the Barbie they were using as a model.

Polly shook her head. "I couldn't. She's yours."

"I've got others. You take her."

Polly stared at Jenny as if she couldn't believe her ears. Then she picked up the doll and began to dress her with the outfit she had made. Jenny glanced at Diane, but she was busy helping Bitsy. Then Jenny looked up as she heard the sound of approaching footsteps. Mr. Carrington was walking down the room toward them with a man and a woman Jenny had never seen before. The man had dark wavy hair and a quick smile, but it was the woman who caught and held Jenny's eye. She was tall with reddish-blonde hair and nearly perfect features. She walked with a lithe grace and was dressed smartly in a soft, beige suit. As the trio approached, the girls became aware of them, and Polly stood up awkwardly, her face flushed. For a moment she and the woman stood facing one another. Then the woman stepped forward and embraced Polly. The other girls looked away, embarrassed but pleased, and they were relieved when the bell sounded, marking the end of the session. Jenny helped with the clean-up, keeping an eye on Polly and the three adults. She saw Polly's mother step back, and then Mr. Carrington said something to Polly, and the man stepped up to her. He held her hand momentarily, then impulsively moved forward and hugged her. The other campers finished their clean-up chores and hurried out, while Diane and Jenny stood to one side and waited. Finally Mr. Carrington turned to them.

"Jenny and Diane, I want you to meet Mr. and Mrs. Carillo. This is Jenny Martin and Diane Drake."

Jenny stepped forward with some trepidition, but the Carillos greeted her warmly. "I owe you a lot, Jenny," Mrs. Carillo said. "Your letter was very important. It helped me make up my mind."

She glanced at her husband, but he shook his head slightly.

"If it's all right with you," he said, turning to Mr. Carrington, "we're going to take Polly to dinner. Just the three of us."

Mr. Carrington smiled. "That sounds like a good idea to me."

Mr. Carillo turned to his wife and Polly. "Shall we go?"

"Wait a minute," Polly said. "I almost forgot."

Stepping over to the table, she picked up the Barbie and brought it to her mother. "I made this for my little sister. I designed and sewed the clothes myself."

Her mother looked at the Barbie closely, then handed it to her husband. "It's beautiful work," she said softly. "Sherry will love it."

"Do you really think she will?" Polly asked.

"Definitely," Mr. Carillo said. "Come on, you two. I'm hungry."

Linking arms with Polly and her mother, he moved quickly up the room.

"It looks good," Mr. Carrington muttered as he watched them go. "Darned if it doesn't look good."

"Do you think they'll take her back with them?" Diane asked. "That's what she's really hoping."

"They might." He turned to Diane, and he was grinning broadly. "Come on, you two. This deserves a good, cold glass of apple cider!"

17 An Unexpected Clue

WHEN Jenny and Billy stepped off the bus the next day, they found an unfamiliar car parked in the driveway. Waving goodbye to Debbie and Drew, they ran to the house, and leaving their schoolbooks on the counter, hurried through to the living room. There they found Mr. and Mrs. Carillo chatting with their mother.

"Hello there," Mr. Carillo greeted them as they stepped into the room. "We probably should have telephoned before dropping by, but we wanted to talk to you, and we didn't realize you got out of school so late."

"Where's Polly?" Jenny asked.

"The last time we saw her, she was in the back yard playing with your dog." Mr. Carillo laughed. "He likes to retrieve things, and she doesn't mind throwing them. I guess they'll keep at it until one or the other tires out."

"Did you have a good supper last night?"

"Very good. It gave us a chance to get to know Polly and visa-versa. We had a lot of catching up to do, and some explaining as well."

"You see, Jenny," Mrs. Carillo said, "it's been an awkward situation. Polly's father was killed in Korea. We had intended to marry, but he had to leave two months earlier than we expected. I took care of Polly until she was school age, but she needed special schooling, and I just couldn't afford it. I arranged through some friends for her to come to Apple Hill, and at first I managed to visit her at least twice a year. Then I met George." She glanced at her husband. "I should have told him about Polly, but I was afraid to, and just the fact of not having told him made it more and more difficult. I tried to come three separate times when I had excuses to fly to New York, but I only made it once. I had to cancel the other trips."

"That's why I wrote," Jenny said softly. "Polly was on top of the world when she thought you were coming. It really hit her when you had to cancel."

"I know. Your letter made me think, and I realized that I had to do something. Things just couldn't go on the way they were going."

"You don't mind that I wrote?"

"Bless you, no. It was just what I needed."

"She told me about Polly that night," Mr. Carillo said, picking up where his wife had left off. "I gave her the dickens for not having told me before, and the next day I arranged for us to come to New York. Polly's quite a girl."

"She really is," Jenny said eagerly. "She's the best one in my group by far, and the other girls really like her. She's just super."

"Well." Mr. Carillo laughed, "I'm afraid you're going to lose her for at least a couple of weeks. We're taking her back to California with us to meet her sisters and brother."

"She must be pleased. She's dying to go to California."

"She is pleased," Mr. Carillo agreed, "but she surprised us, and Mr. Carrington, too. She wants to come back here to serve as a counselor. We were taken aback at first, but I think we understand now. She feels a real commitment to Apple Hill. Of course, she'll visit with us frequently, and if she should change her mind, she'll certainly have a home with us."

"She won't," Jenny assured him. "I know Polly. Once she makes up her mind about something, it stays made up. What did Mr. Carrington say?"

"He said he'd be delighted to take Polly on. We'll talk to him after this trip." He looked up, hearing a door close in the distance. Seconds later, Polly strolled into the room, followed by Skipper. Seeing Jenny,

Skipper hurried over, as if to demonstrate that his shift of allegiance was only temporary.

"So who got tired first," Mr. Carillo asked. "You or the dog?"

Polly laughed. "Both of us. He's really cute, Jenny. It's the first time I've had a chance to play with him."

"Ready for California, Pol?" Billy asked.

Polly grinned, smiling at her newfound parents. "I'm ready."

"Is it as warm out there as Polly says?" Jenny asked, turning to Mrs. Carillo.

"It never gets very cold where we are," Mrs. Carillo allowed. "I think we're going to have to get Polly some warm-weather clothes."

"I don't think she'll mind that," Jenny said, glancing at Polly. "I'll bet you won't miss the cold mornings."

Polly smiled back, but her tone when she spoke was serious. "No, I won't miss the cold mornings, but I will miss the fireplaces. A fireplace seems to make everything warm and comfy. It seems like a house isn't a house without a fireplace and chimney. Apple Hill has the biggest fireplace I've ever seen."

"That's it!" Billy exclaimed suddenly. He turned to Jenny. "Remember what John Quarry told us about burying the Bible and *something of value*. That's what he meant!"

Everyone turned to Billy, but he was staring at Jenny.

"What are you talking about, Billy?" Mrs. Martin

asked, watching her son with a puzzled expression.

"It's the clue, Mom. It's what Jenny and I have been trying to think of. John Quarry talked about burying a Bible and *something of value* next to the chimney. What Polly said about the chimney and the fireplace at Apple Hill reminded me."

Mrs. Martin stared at Billy, shaking her head. "We'll talk about it later," she said finally, and turning to the Carillos, told them briefly about the Quarry gang and the recent aftermath of their story. "If you ask me," she concluded, "the money was taken and spent long ago, but I suppose wherever money is concerned, people tend to be eternal optimists."

"That's true," Mr. Carillo agreed. He glanced at his watch and then stood up. "We'd better be off," he said. "We have to collect Polly's things at Apple Hill, and we've got a plane to catch."

Thanking Mrs. Martin for her hospitality, he led the way to the back door. Before leaving, Mrs. Carillo turned to Jenny.

"Jenny, I want you to know how grateful we are. Perhaps you can visit us some day in California."

"I'd like that."

Shaking her hand, Mr. Carillo stepped outside. Mrs. Carillo followed, after first embracing Jenny; and then Polly and Jenny exchanged a warm hug. The Martins stood in the doorway watching, while the Carillos climbed into their rented car and backed out of the driveway.

On the way back to the living room, Billy asked Jenny what she thought about his idea.

Jenny turned to her mother. "What do you think, Mom?"

"I think it depends on your impression of John Quarry," Mrs. Martin said slowly, resuming her seat on the sofa. "Think back and ask yourself *how* he said it. Did he seem to be calling attention to it?"

"He wouldn't have done that. Wes might have picked up on it."

Mrs. Martin looked at her son. "Wesley Garavoy?"

Billy nodded. "The thing he seemed to be emphasizing was the Bible. He said it might not seem like much, but maybe there was more to it than met the eye."

"He was talking about the poem," Jenny said.

"Maybe, and maybe not. I think we ought to tell Captain Wiley. It wouldn't take him long to check the foundation of the chimney in John Quarry's cabin. Then, if he doesn't find it there, he can check the chimney in the old farmhouse at Apple Hill."

"Billy's right," Mrs. Martin decided. "Call Captain Wiley right now. He should still be at his office."

Jenny watched as Billy left the room to make the call. In spite of herself, she had a feeling that Billy might be right, and she was irritated that she hadn't thought of it. It had just slipped by. He had said it in the course of conversation, and she had made no particular note of it. But Billy's reasoning was good. If John Quarry *had* underlined it, Wes might have caught on. And after all, John Quarry had asked Billy to bring him the Bible. He had set it up so he could say what he had said. Yes, Billy just might be right.

18 Discovery

JENNY and Billy were about to leave Apple Hill the next afternoon with Drew and Debbie when Mr. Drake called and told them that Mr. Carrington wanted to see them. Drew and Debbie decided to go on home, but Jenny and Billy followed across the lawn to the old farmhouse in which Mr. Carrington lived and had his office. He was waiting for them, and they walked quickly into his study. Captain Wiley was sitting in the chair by the desk. He grinned as he noted their surprise.

"Didn't expect to see me here, did you? Fact is, Billy's idea sounded pretty good to me, and I've been busy."

"Have you found anything?"

"We excavated the area around John Quarry's chimney and found a Bible and a gold piece. I've been telling Mr. Carrington about the two poems and what you recall Quarry saying."

"Did John Quarry say anything directly about Apple Hill?" Mr. Carrington asked.

"No, he didn't," Jenny replied.

"But the second poem mentions Apple Hill," Billy added.

"It could be intended to mislead us, of course," Captain Wiley noted. "I've considered that, and that's why I haven't come here before."

"You say that Ed Quarry used to stay here often?" Mr. Drake asked.

"Wes Garavoy says he used to stay here as often as he stayed with John Quarry on the mountain," Billy replied. "Then he almost got caught, and he didn't come back again."

"So you think the money may be buried in the cellar of this house." Mr. Carrington stared out the window, a faint smile playing at the corners of his mouth. "It's ironic in a way. All the problems we've had raising money, and if you're right, we may have been sitting on a fortune all the time."

"If the money is here, what will happen to it?" Jenny asked, turning to Captain Wiley.

"That's for the town to decide, but I imagine it will be split between Apple Hill, the town, and the state, once any surviving claims have been paid off."

"What do you propose?" Mr. Carrington asked, turning away from the window.

"Let's go down to the cellar and have a look. I think it's just possible that John Quarry was giving us a verbal clue to go along with two written clues. It would be like him. He figured if we were smart enough to pick up on it, we would deserve what we found, and if we weren't, then the money would be lost forever. I think he would have been just as glad if it was never found, but he liked a game, and he was a gambler. I suspect it pleased him to think that he had left this puzzle for us to chew on. It may have pleased him, too, to think that he was making Jenny and Billy a free gift of the solution to the puzzle."

"That is, if they had the wit to see it," Mr. Drake corrected.

"Good point." Captain Wiley stood up and started for the door. "Let's go."

They left the office quickly, and Mr. Carrington led the way down to the basement. The cellar was large and deep. Part of the floor was concrete, and on it was an oil-burning furnace and a hot water heater.

"Did you put in the concrete?" Captain Wiley asked.

"It was here when we bought the place. We converted from coal to oil and replaced the water heater, but otherwise we've made no changes."

"Do you have shovels?"

Mr. Carrington nodded, pointing to three spades in

the corner. Captain Wiley took out a walkie-talkie and spoke into it. Then he returned it to his pocket and stepped over to the chimney base, studying the brick foundation carefully. When his men arrived, he pointed to the spades and told them where he wanted them to dig. They started at once and worked steadily, digging around the base of the chimney. Ten minutes later there was a solid *thunk* of metal encountering metal. The digger whose spade had hit something turned to the other man, who joined him, and the two dug at a furious pace.

"It's a good-sized box," one of them said over his shoulder. "We should have it clear pretty soon."

Five minutes later they climbed into the trench and lifted the box out. It was a foot high, a foot and a half wide, and two feet long. Captain Wiley inspected it closely, then turned to the others.

"Well, this looks like it. It's locked, and I'm not going to try to open it until I get to the bank." He motioned for one of his men to come closer. "Call Gus and tell him I'm on the way over. I want at least three bank officers present." He glanced at Mr. Carrington. "Are you going to be at the Town Meeting tonight?"

"I wouldn't miss it. In fact, I'm coming with everyone on my staff who can be spared. I've heard rumors that some things of concern to us may be brought up."

"I wouldn't be surprised." Captain Wiley looked down at the box. Then he turned to Jenny and Billy. "Can I give you two a lift home?"

"Yes, please," Jenny replied.

After giving his men instructions, Captain Wiley watched while they carried the box upstairs and loaded it into the police van. Then, satisfied that it was safe, he led the way to his own car.

"I was right about the Bible thing, wasn't I?" Billy observed as they drove out of the driveway.

"You sure were, Billy."

"Think there's money in the box, or things that they stole?"

Captain Wiley glanced at Billy quickly before returning his eyes to the road. "Money, I'd guess."

"How much?"

"No way to know, but the box seemed pretty heavy."

Billy whistled. "Money's not too heavy. It would take a lot to make that box heavy."

"Oh, a fair bit." Captain Wiley looked up in the mirror, so that he could see both their faces. "Say a few hundred thousand, more or less."

This time Jenny whistled, too.

19 Town Meeting

THE high school gymnasium was packed. Every seat was taken, and there were at least fifty people standing against the walls when the Dover Valley Town Meeting was called to order that night. Behind a long table in the front of the room were the three Selectmen, the town medical officer, the First Selectman's secretary, and a county representative. There was also an empty chair marked Town Constable, which Mr. Martin explained to Jenny and Billy was reserved for Captain Wiley as Chief of Police. Minutes of the previous meeting and the report of the town treasurer had been handed out at the door, and the first part of the meeting was occupied with questions on these and some financial explanations, dealing with a bond issue, which Jenny and Billy found hard to follow. Then there was extended discussion about garbage collection. Finally, Jacob Colburn, the First Selectman, brought up the matter of straightening Paxton Road to eliminate the "S" curve. He explained that the project had been under consideration for some time, and that former Selectman Gene Crabtree had obtained plans from the state highway department that would require the condemnation of a portion of the Garavoy property.

There was a buzz of excitement as he said this, and eyes turned to Wes and Lee Garavoy, who were standing midway down the room on the right. Mr. Colburn went on to explain that the Garavoy house would have to be moved to another part of the property, adding that the move would, of course, be made at state expense. He described briefly the benefits rerouting would bring, and then asked for comments. Jenny looked expectantly at Wes, but to her surprise, it was not Wes, but her own father who stood up to speak.

"Mr. Colburn and fellow citizens," he began. "I spoke to Wes and Lee Garavoy about the matter, and I am now speaking for them as well as for myself. The state proposal to straighten Paxton Road would involve not only the dislocation of the Garavoy house, but considerable blasting as well. We feel that there is a good alternative that has not been given proper consideration. We think the road should follow Tooks Creek from where it first crosses Paxton Road to where it crosses again a quarter mile past the "S" curve. The route would be flatter and straighter, no blasting would be required, and no houses would have to be moved. We think these are important considerations."

The First Selectman turned to one of his colleagues, and they spoke briefly in whispers. Then he turned to face the room.

"Any comment on that, Mr. Crabtree?"

Mr. Crabtree stood up. He was in the third row on the end. "To answer Mr. Martin, the state engineer and I did consider routing Paxton Road next to Tooks Creek and decided against if for three reasons. It would take longer to complete than the proposed cut through the Garavoy property. It would spoil some good grazing land and disrupt watering arrangements for the farmers along the brook, and it would require a considerable amount of fill."

"Would it be cheaper?" Mr. Colburn asked.

Mr. Crabtree hesitated. "That would depend on the amount of blasting required."

"In other words, we need cost estimates on both routes."

Again Mr. Colburn leaned over to confer with his colleague. Then he turned to the Third Selectman and spoke briefly to him.

"We've decided to table the matter, pending cost estimates," he announced finally. "However, let me say that as of this moment, we incline to the route along Tooks Creek, providing it's not out of line financially. We don't like to interfere with citizens' rights unless we have to in this town. In short, we approve the objective, but we want longer to consider the means. Will all in favor of tabling the matter pending further study raise their hands?"

The show of hands was nearly unanimous, and Jenny noted that Wes was smiling and Lee looked less grim than usual. A moment later, however, Wes's smile became a frown, and Jenny turned to find Mr. Crabtree again on his feet.

"Mr. Colburn, I would like to raise another matter for the consideration of this meeting. Apple Hill Foundation, Inc. came to this town eleven years ago. As a non-profit foundation, they were exempted from local taxes and set up operations on the Apple Hill property, which was deeded to them by Mrs. Walker Carey. Over the eleven years since, Apple Hill has expanded considerably, and the process appears to be continuing. I suggest that it's time the citizens of Dover Valley reappraised Apple Hill's position in this community and our attitude toward it. Specifically I see two areas for discussion. First, I have a state health examiner's report here that indicates the present sanitary facilities are inadequate for an institution of its size."

"Let me stop you there for a moment," Mr. Colburn interrupted. "Is Mr. Carrington present?"

"Yes."

Jenny looked over her shoulder and saw the Carringtons, the Drakes, and the Smarts sitting together near the back of the room.

"Are you aware of the report to which Mr. Crabtree is referring?"

"We are. The trustees voted funds two days ago to build a new facility for waste disposal. Work will start next month."

Mr. Colburn nodded, gesturing to his secretary to bring him a folder. He opened it and glanced at the contents. "I have Apple Hill's specifications here, and I find them in order. Mr. Crabtree?"

Mr. Crabtree stood up again, and Jenny sensed a stir of anticipation. Evidently, some people were expecting fireworks, but they did not come. Mr. Crabtree was if anything more calm and low-key than he had been before.

"Mr. Carrington has me there," he admitted, glancing back at the Apple Hill group with a tight smile, "but I submit that the problem I am suggesting goes much deeper than building a new sanitation facility. Apple Hill Farm is located in an area that is residentially zoned. Initially there was no problem with this, since Apple Hill was comparatively small, but that has changed. Apple Hill has grown in size and is still growing. The farm is producing increasingly large quantities of food products and the workshops are manufacturing furniture, pots, and other items for sale. In other words, the Apple Hill property is operating *as a business* geared to sell as much as possible *at the farm.* That is, of course, technically in violation of zoning. Even more it is unfair competition to the other farms of the community. They are competing against local farmers to sell produce within the community, but they have the advantage of paying no taxes and of selling goods on their premises. If you consider that Apple Hill avails itself of many facilities provided at community expense such as schools, busing, fire protection and police, you begin to see that the community is being forced to subsidize Apple Hill without ever having made a formal decision to that effect. I think this is a serious issue, and I think many of the people in this room share my objection to this *de facto* subsidization of Apple Hill Farm. Whether or not it is worthy *is not* the issue; whether this community should sign a blank check *is* the issue. I propose that our Selectmen set up a committee to study this issue and report back to us in thirty days time with their conclusions."

Mr. Crabtree sat down to limited applause and some booing; there was an immediate buzz of conversation. In the middle of it, Captain Wiley appeared at the side door and worked his way to the front. He spoke briefly to the First Selectman, then sat down in the chair behind the Town Constable sign. Jenny watched him closely, but his face was expressionless. Then she looked to her left as the crowd quieted, and a woman stood up to speak. The woman took sharp exception to Mr. Crabtree's suggestion, arguing that Apple Hill had proved a good neighbor, and that the town services it used were more than offset by the buying that Apple Hill did within the community. After she had finished, several other people spoke, both for and against Apple Hill. To Jenny's surprise, none of the Apple Hill people volunteered to speak. When she asked her father about this, he explained that it was a better tactic for them not to speak unless they were asked specific questions, as they had been on the matter of the sewage plant. Finally Mr. Colburn ended the discussion, saying that he would set up a committee, chaired by himself, to consider the relationship between Apple Hill and the community.

"Will all in favor of forming such a committee for that purpose please raise their hands?"

Again the show of hands was virtually unanimous. Mr. Colburn said something to his secretary, and then, holding up his hands for silence, asked if there was any further business. When no one spoke, he turned to Captain Wiley, saying that the Town Constable had an announcement to make.

To Jenny it seemed as if everyone in the room began to talk at once while Mr. Colburn was sitting down and Captain Wiley was getting to his feet. Rumors about the death of Heineken and the Quarry loot had been circulating actively, and there was an undertone of excitement everywhere. Captain Wiley stood for a moment without speaking, waiting for the crowd to quiet down. Jenny glanced at Billy, but he was staring straight ahead, his eyes fixed on Captain Wiley. She turned back as the Captain began to speak.

"There have been a lot of rumors going around this

past month. I've been aware of them, but I wasn't in a position to give you a report. Now I am. Kurt Heineken was parolled two months ago and returned to Dover Valley. He got together with his cousin, Greg Smith, and the two of them attempted to discover where the money acquired by the Quarry gang from stolen goods had been hidden. In the course of their efforts they were killed, along with John Quarry, when the old mine shaft collapsed, trapping them inside."

"How come John Quarry got killed with them?" someone called from the back of the room.

"We think he was helping them look for the Quarry money."

"Is it buried in the mine?" called another voice.

"No. It was buried on Apple Hill Farm, and we've found it."

The tidal wave of sound that followed this announcement took some time to recede. Captain Wiley waited it out, standing motionless, a slight smile playing at the corners of his mouth. Finally one voice made itself heard above the others, asking how much money had been found. The crowd fell silent, waiting for Captain Wiley's reply.

"We'll have to verify the total, but it appears to be approximately four hundred thousand dollars."

A chorus of whistles and exclamations followed, and again it was some time before it subsided. Captain Wiley conferred briefly with Mr. Colburn during the interval, then held his hand up for silence.

"I've spoken to the Selectmen about how we will dispose of the money. First we will pay all surviving insurance and any other bonafide claims. The money that remains after those payments are made will go into the town treasury with the understanding that a portion yet to be determined will be paid to the state and another portion to Apple Hill Farm, since the money was found on their property and with their cooperation." He paused momentarily, his eyes sweeping the audience. "There remains one other matter. Along with the money we found a statement, signed by Ed Quarry, naming the individual who fenced the stolen goods for him. We expect to arrest that individual soon. I might add that circumstantial evidence suggests that that same individual killed Ed Quarry. In other words, the Quarry mystery, which has continued to baffle us over a twelve-year period, appears finally to have been fully solved."

There were several questions after that, but the answers added nothing new. Finally Captain Wiley sat down, and the meeting was officially closed by Mr. Colburn. Although many people stayed to talk and gossip, the Martins left quickly, hurrying out to the parking lot with Mr. Martin leading the way. He stopped abruptly, however, long before reaching their car, and Jenny, who was walking behind him, almost ran into him.

"Why did you stop?" she asked.

"Look."

Just ahead of them Mr. Crabtree was standing by his car, unlocking the door. As they watched, two policemen moved up, one on either side of him. They had linked their arms in his before he was even aware of them. He spoke sharply, trying to pull loose, but they held him tightly. People leaving the meeting had stopped to stare, and Mr. Crabtree evidently decided against further resistance. Jenny saw his face briefly as he was led away. There was no color. His eyes were rolling, and his body was limp. He looked sick, and it was hard to believe that this was the same man who had stood up before the town meeting twenty minutes before.

"Do you think they're arresting him?" Jenny asked in a whisper.

"Looks that way."

"Then that means . . ."

"Exactly. He used to be in the antique business." Mr. Martin turned away, shaking his head. "I always wondered how Crabtree got his money. I guess now we know."

20 A Surprise for Billy

The next day when Jenny and Billy came home from school, they found Wes and Lee Garavoy talking to their father on the back porch. Skipper ran to meet the children, and after petting him, they stepped over to join the three men.

"Good news," Wes told them as they walked up. "Mr. Colburn passed the word to your father that they've decided against straightening the road by moving our house. They talked to the engineer. Seems Crabtree sold him a bill of goods about legal obstacles. The engineer says the route along the creek would make a lot more sense."

"Why did Mr. Crabtree do that?" Billy asked.

"It's hard to say, but I think the man who can answer that question is just driving up."

Jenny and Billy turned in time to see Captain Wiley's car pull into the driveway. Captain Wiley paused to light a cigar, then slid out and walked over to join them.

"Billy was just asking me why Crabtree was so anxious to put that road through our place, Gil," Wes asked. "You got any ideas?"

Captain Wiley bent down to pet Skipper. Then he stood up and stretched. "Couple of reasons. He thought the Quarry money was either at Apple Hill or on your place. He knew it wasn't in the graveyard house because he had searched that, and I think he managed to search John Quarry's house four years ago when John was in the hospital with a broken leg. He figured that if it was at your house and you knew about it, you'd try to bribe him when he put the pressure on."

"How could he have thought we had the money? We've never had a dime to spend."

"He figured you might have been lying low until Heineken was out of the way. The way he saw it, you two might just disappear someday and the money with you. Either that, or the money was in your house and you didn't know it. He thought he'd get in and have a look when they were getting ready to move the house."

"Guess that's why he tried to buy Apple Hill, too."

"Right. That was the place Ed Quarry stayed most often, and Crabtree thought Ed had probably buried the money in the old farmhouse, only there was no way he could get at it as long as the Carringtons were living there."

"So he was the fence." Wes looked down at the ground, shaking his head. "Lee figured there was some tie-in between him and Quarry, but I couldn't see it."

"You never do listen," Lee muttered darkly. Wes gave him a sharp look, but did not respond, turning instead to Captain Wiley.

"Was Crabtree fencing for Quarry from the beginning?"

"Right from the start. It was a perfect set-up actually. He bought and sold antiques in his own shop in New York City and to other dealers out of state. My guess is that he planned the operation with Ed Quarry. Quarry met him through Heineken, and once Ed learned that Crabtree was in the antique business, he suggested they work together. They kept it between themselves, according to Crabtree. Heineken didn't even know, although he kept trying to find out."

"Did Crabtree kill Ed Quarry?" Mr. Martin asked.

Captain Wiley nodded. "He wouldn't admit it at first, but when we showed him a copy of Ed's written statement, he did. Ed pretty well fingered him."

"Why did he kill Ed?" Wes asked.

"He didn't mean to. If we can believe him, and I think we can, it was self-defense. You see, Ed was planning to leave the country. Crabtree had obtained a counterfeit passport and boat tickets for him. Ed's plan was to pack up the money and go somewhere in South America to start a new life. On that final day Crabtree was supposed to meet Ed in the house by the graveyard, bringing the passport and the tickets. What Crabtree didn't know was that Ed planned to kill him, so there would be no chance of anyone's learning his new name or where he was going. Remember that he had already turned in Heineken, and Heineken was locked away for a minimum of ten years. He planned to kill Crabtree, dig up the money at Apple Hill, which was still deserted then, catch his boat, and disappear."

"That was what Crabtree told you?"

"Partly, and partly what I've figured out. Crabtree says he gave the passport and tickets to Ed and asked for the money that Ed was supposed to be paying for them. Instead of giving him the money, Ed pulled a gun, but Crabtree had smelled a rat and brought his own gun just in case. He was ready for Ed, and when Ed pulled the gun, Crabtree flipped the table and got behind it. Ed shot over his head, and Crabtree killed him. He tells me he had learned to shoot a pistol when he was in the army, and he had kept in practice. Anyhow, that was that for Quarry. He was killed instantly, which meant that Crabtree had no way to discover where Ed had hidden the money. Ever since then he's been trying to find it."

"Why didn't he go to John Quarry?" Mr. Martin asked.

"He didn't dare. He was afraid the old man would turn him in."

"What do you think will happen about Apple Hill now that Mr. Crabtree's not going to be around any more?" Jenny asked.

"I expect they'll drop the whole business. Most people think Apple Hill's a good thing. You kids have been helping a lot, talking about Apple Hill to your friends. Besides, Crabtree never had that many people on his side to begin with. Hey," he added, turning to Billy, "I came over here for a reason. I only told you part of the truth the other day, and it's time I told you the rest."

Captain Wiley was grinning broadly, and he waited on purpose, letting the suspense build up, his eyes fixed on Billy. Finally Jenny could stand it no longer and asked what he meant.

"Remember I told you that we found a Bible and a gold coin when we dug around the base of John Quarry's chimney? Well, that wasn't all we found."

"What did you find?" Jenny asked, her voice barely audible.

"We found a strongbox, and in it thirty-three thousand dollars in cash. Since John Quarry has no other heirs of whom we're aware, and since he named you his heir in front of an independent witness, you, Billy, will receive thirty-three thousand dollars, less taxes, probate costs and so on. I didn't want to say anything the other day, because I thought it might have been

Ed Quarry's money, but now that we've found what we've found at Apple Hill, that seems to clear the tracks. How does it feel to be an heir?"

Captain Wiley smiled at Billy, who stared back at him, too amazed to react. Indeed all three Martins, and the Garavoys as well, were too startled to speak. Mr. Martin repeated the figure, shaking his head in disbelief, while Jenny moved next to Billy, and Skipper, sensing that something important was happening, but puzzled as to what it was, stood at his feet. It was Lee, oddly, who was the first to move. He stepped forward and took Billy's hand in both of his, muttering congratulations in a low, embarrassed voice. Then Wes threw an arm around Billy's shoulders and gave him a squeeze.

"What are you going to do with all that money, Billy?" he asked.

Billy laughed. "I don't know. I guess I'll let Mom and Dad figure that out for me." He glanced at his father. "Maybe I can use it for college, me and Jenny both."

"We'll see." Mr. Martin turned to Captain Wiley. "Thanks, Gil."

"Don't thank me. Thank John Quarry."

"I wish I could," Billy said softly. "I liked him. Hey, Wes, you and Lee should get some of that money. I wouldn't have even met John Quarry if it hadn't been for you."

Wes shook his head. "No way. Lee and me wouldn't know what to do with any extra money, would we, Lee?"

Lee gave one of his rare laughs. "I might be able to figure out something," he allowed.

They all laughed at this, and Lee waited for the laughter to subside before adding that he'd rather see Billy have the money.

"I guess that's it then," Captain Wiley summed up. "The Quarry gang's no more; the money has been recovered; Wes and Lee won't have to move their house; Apple Hill is safe; and Billy and Jenny have money for college. I'd call that a fair fall's work."

If any punctuation were needed, two sharp barks from Skipper put the cap on it. The Quarry mystery was indeed laid to rest.

ISBN 0-689-30897-3 $9.95

Jenny and Billy have just moved to Dover Valley, so when new friends tell them that Kurt Heineken of the Quarry gang has been released from prison it doesn't mean much. Not until a few days later, when they are exploring an old graveyard atop nearby Dover Mountain and see a man they are sure is Heineken, does the story of the Quarry gang, its robberies and its murders, seem important. Then, suddenly, they are thrust into the twelve-year-old mystery of who killed the head of the gang, Ed Quarry, and where he hid the loot the gang had amassed. They still have time, however, to get jobs as junior counselors at a neighboring farm, Apple Hill, which houses and trains retarded young people.

But Apple Hill, too, seems to be a part of the mystery, because Ed Quarry spent time at the then-vacant farm. And for some reason, another local resident seems to want to do away with the program now in operation at the farm. Does this have anything to do with the missing money, or the question of Quarry's death?

How John Quarry did meet his end, what did happen to the loot, and what happens to Heineken and to Apple Hill all combine to make this an exciting story.

812;46